DISCARD

HAN SOLO AND THE
HOLLOW MOON OF KHORYA

visit us at www.abdopublishing.com

Reinforced library bound edition published in 2012 by Spotlight, a division of the ABDO Group, 8000 West 78th Street, Edina, Minnesota 55439.
Spotlight produces high-quality reinforced library bound editions for schools and libraries. Published by agreement with Dark Horse Comics, Inc., and Lucasfilm Ltd.
Printed in the United States of America, Melrose Park, Illinois.

052010
092010

♻ This book contains at least 10% recycled materials.

Special thanks to Elaine Mederer, Jann Moorhead, David Anderman, Leland Chee, Sue Rostoni, and Carol Roeder at Lucas Licensing

Cataloging-in-Publication Data

Barlow, Jeremy.
Star wars adventures: Han Solo and the hollow moon of Khorya /
  by Jeremy Barlow ; pencils Rick Lacy ; inks Matthew Loux ; colors Michael Atiyeh ;
  lettering Michael Heisler ; cover art Rich Lacy and Michael Atiyeh. -- Reinforced library bound ed.
  p. cm. -- (Star Wars Adventures)
Summary: In this action-packed tale, Han and Chewie are caught between gangsters and the Empire, and their only help is Han's former partner--who may be worse than either!
1. Solo, Han (Fictitious character)--Fiction. 2. Comic books, strips, etc. 3. Star Wars fiction.
4. Chewbacca (Fictitious character)--Comic books, strips, etc. 5. Graphic novels.
6. Science fiction comic books, strips, etc.
I. Lacy, Rick. II. Loux, Matthew. III. Title.
[741.5'973]--dc22
ISBN 978-1-59961-900-2 (reinforced library bound edition)

All Spotlight books are reinforced library bindings
and manufactured in the United States of America.

HAN SOLO AND THE
HOLLOW MOON OF KHORYA

3 1389 02074 7416

Script **Jeremy Barlow**

Pencils **Rick Lacy**

Inks **Matthew Loux**

Colors **Michael Atiyeh**

Lettering **Michael Heisler**

Cover art **Rick Lacy and Michael Atiyeh**

Dark Horse Books®

THIS STORY TAKES PLACE APPROXIMATELY ONE YEAR BEFORE STAR WARS: A NEW HOPE.

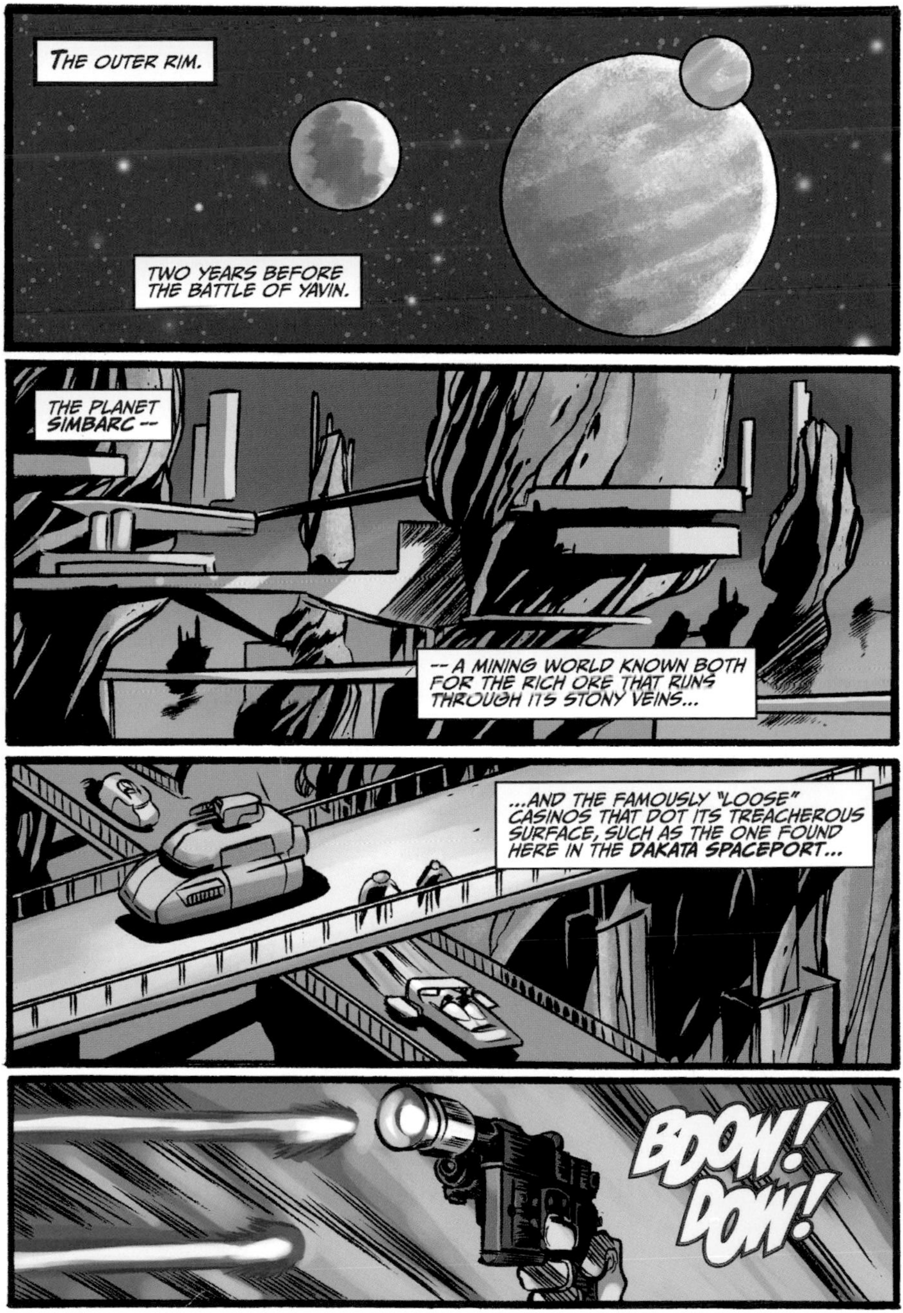
THE OUTER RIM.
TWO YEARS BEFORE THE BATTLE OF YAVIN.
THE PLANET SIMBARC --
-- A MINING WORLD KNOWN BOTH FOR THE RICH ORE THAT RUNS THROUGH ITS STONY VEINS...
...AND THE FAMOUSLY "LOOSE" CASINOS THAT DOT ITS TREACHEROUS SURFACE, SUCH AS THE ONE FOUND HERE IN THE DAKATA SPACEPORT...
BDOW! DOW!

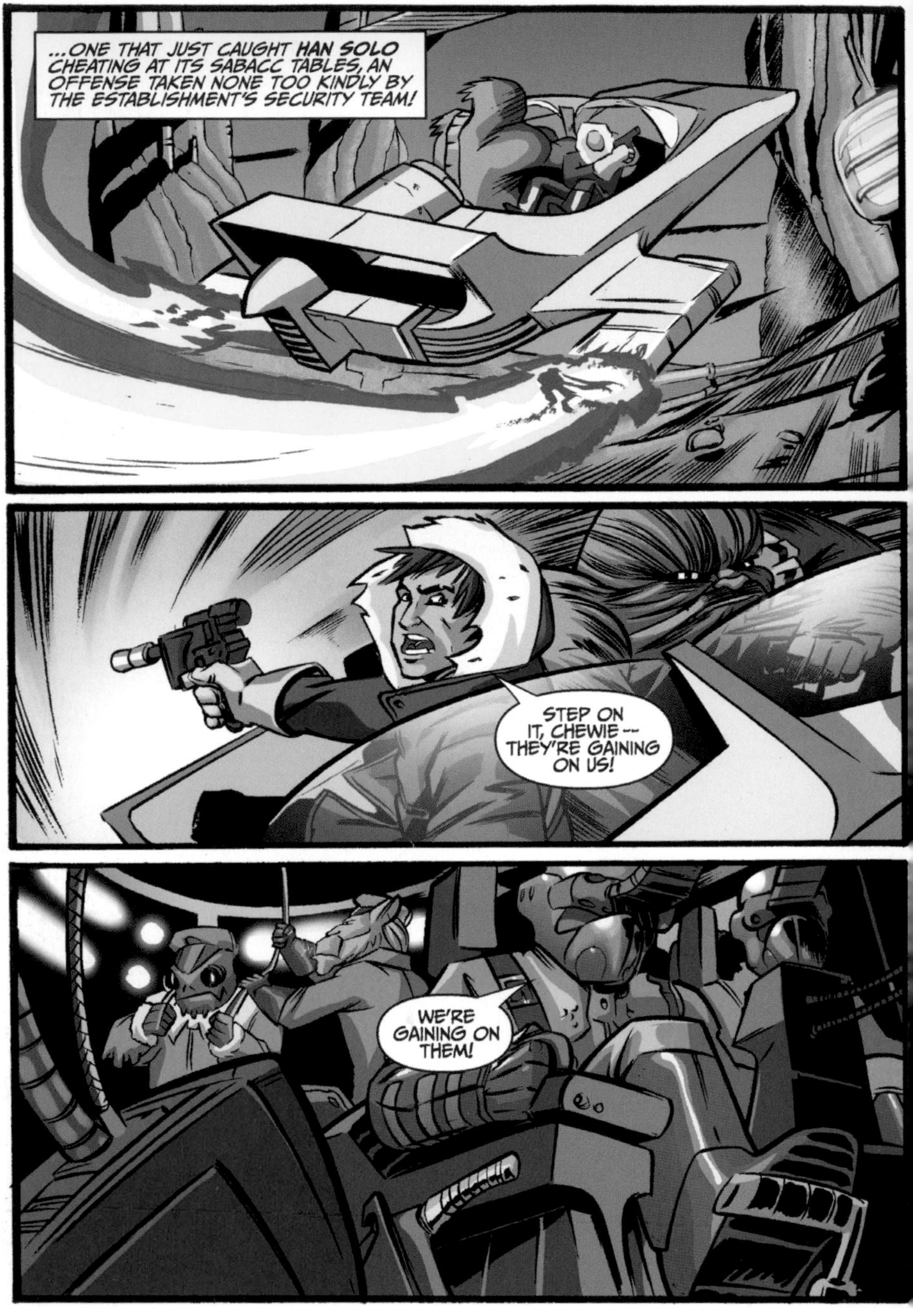
...ONE THAT JUST CAUGHT HAN SOLO CHEATING AT ITS SABACC TABLES, AN OFFENSE TAKEN NONE TOO KINDLY BY THE ESTABLISHMENT'S SECURITY TEAM!
STEP ON IT, CHEWIE -- THEY'RE GAINING ON US!
WE'RE GAINING ON THEM!

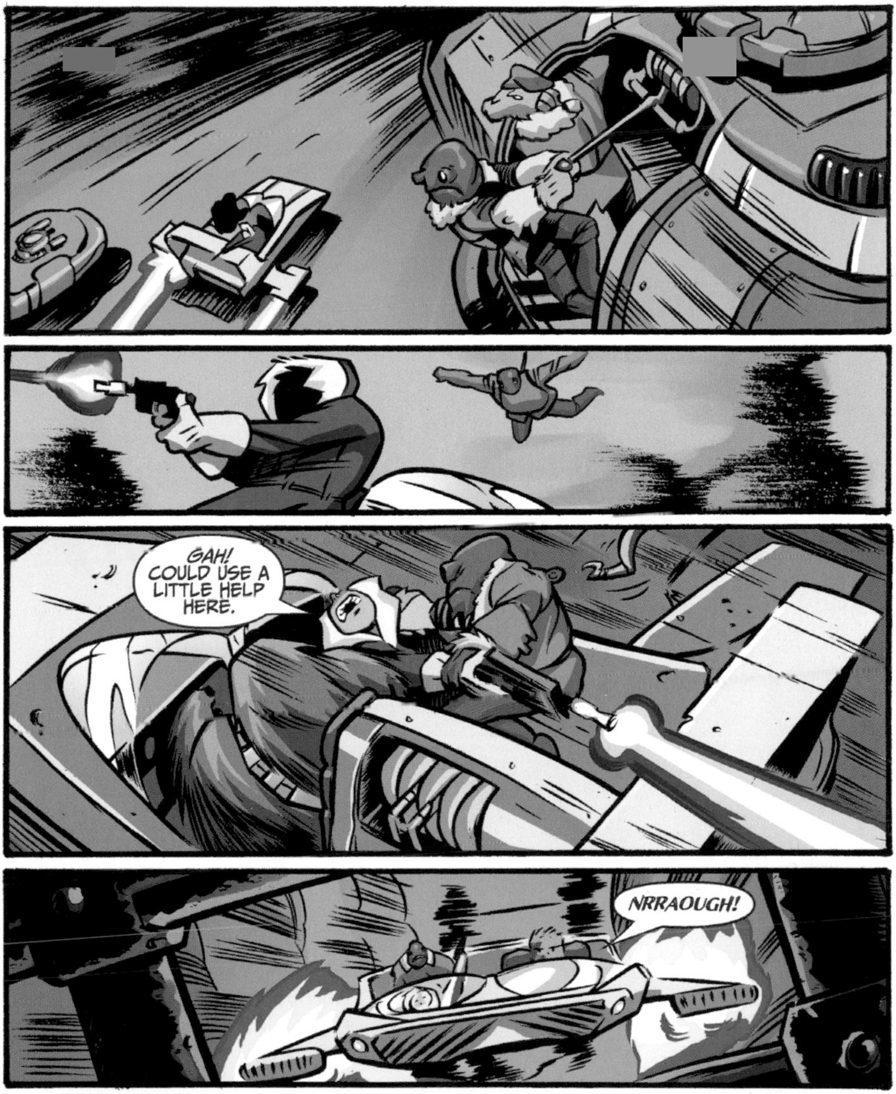
GAH! COULD USE A LITTLE HELP HERE.
NRRAOUGH!
CHEWIE...?

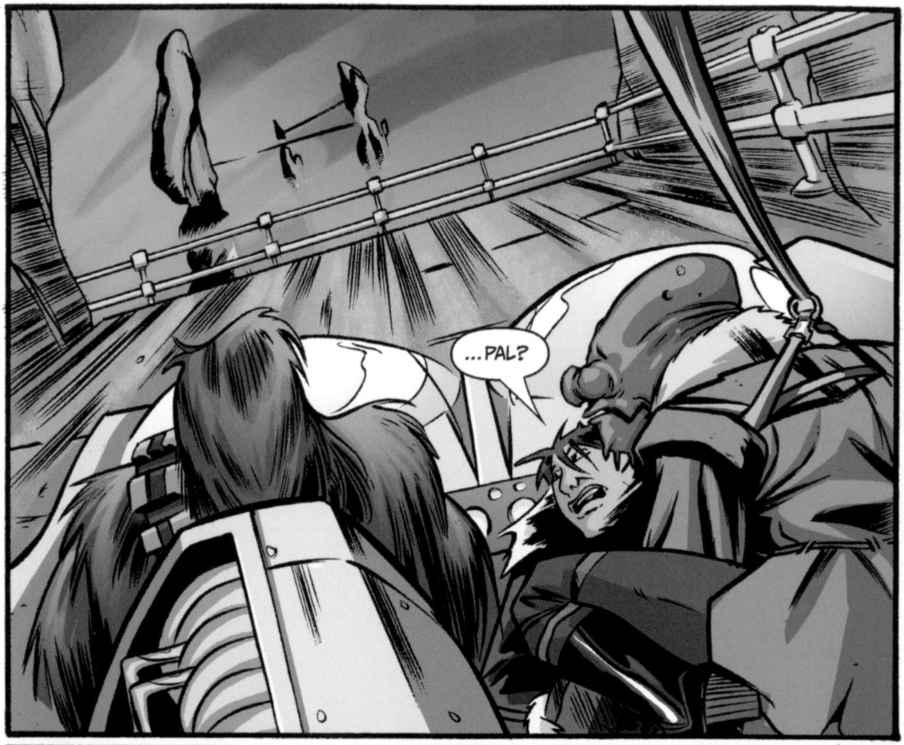
...PAL?

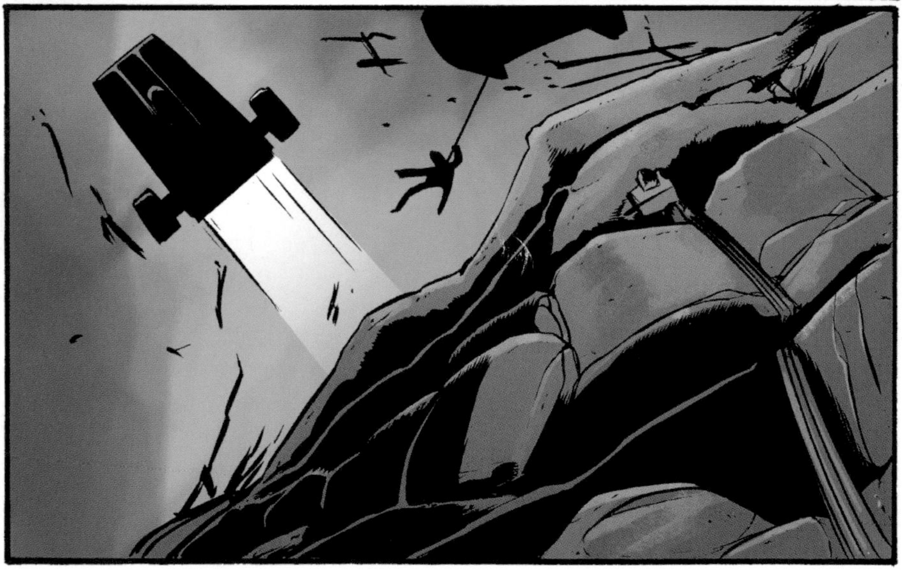

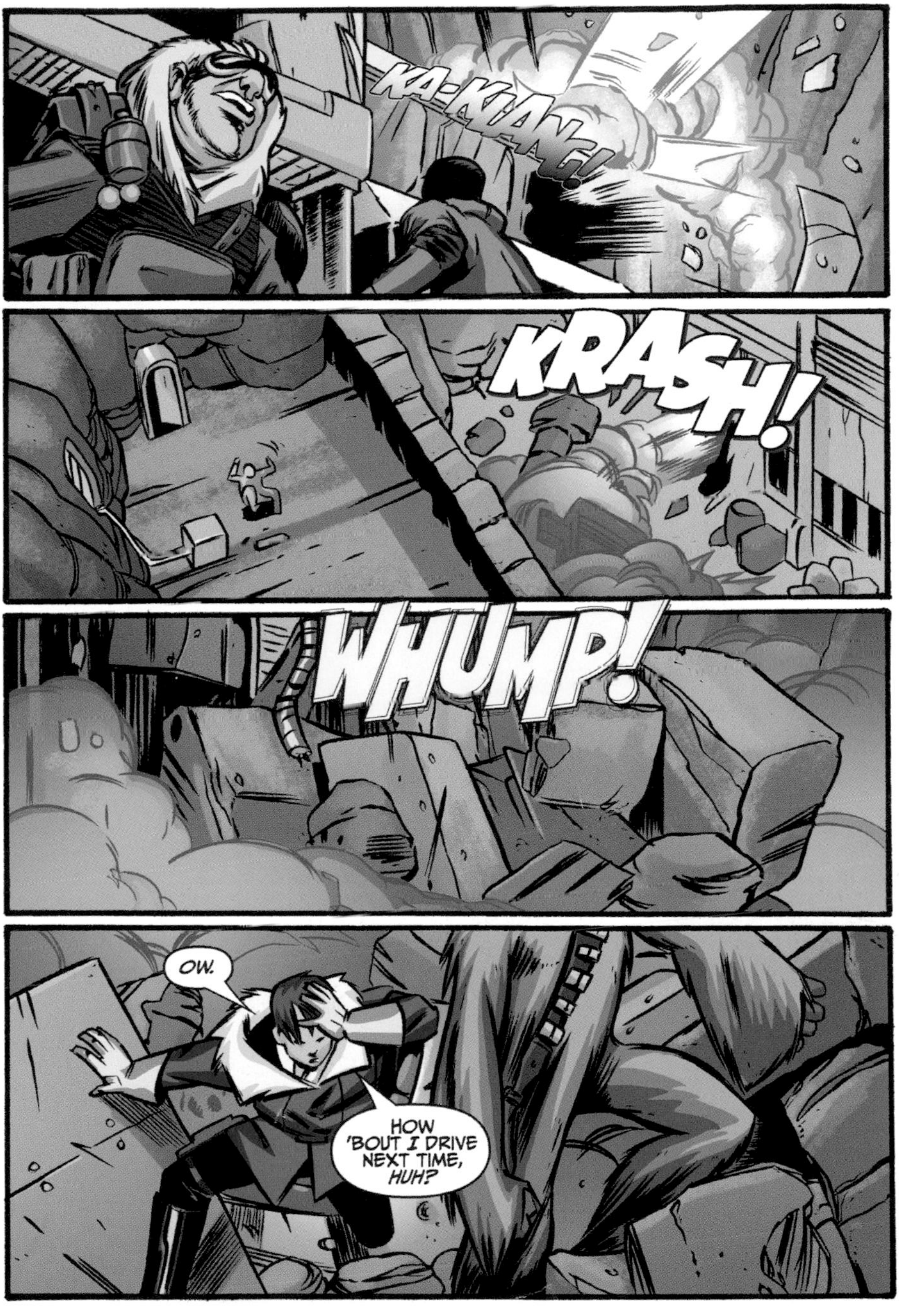
KA-KLANG!
KRASH!
WHUMP!
OW.
HOW 'BOUT I DRIVE NEXT TIME, HUH?

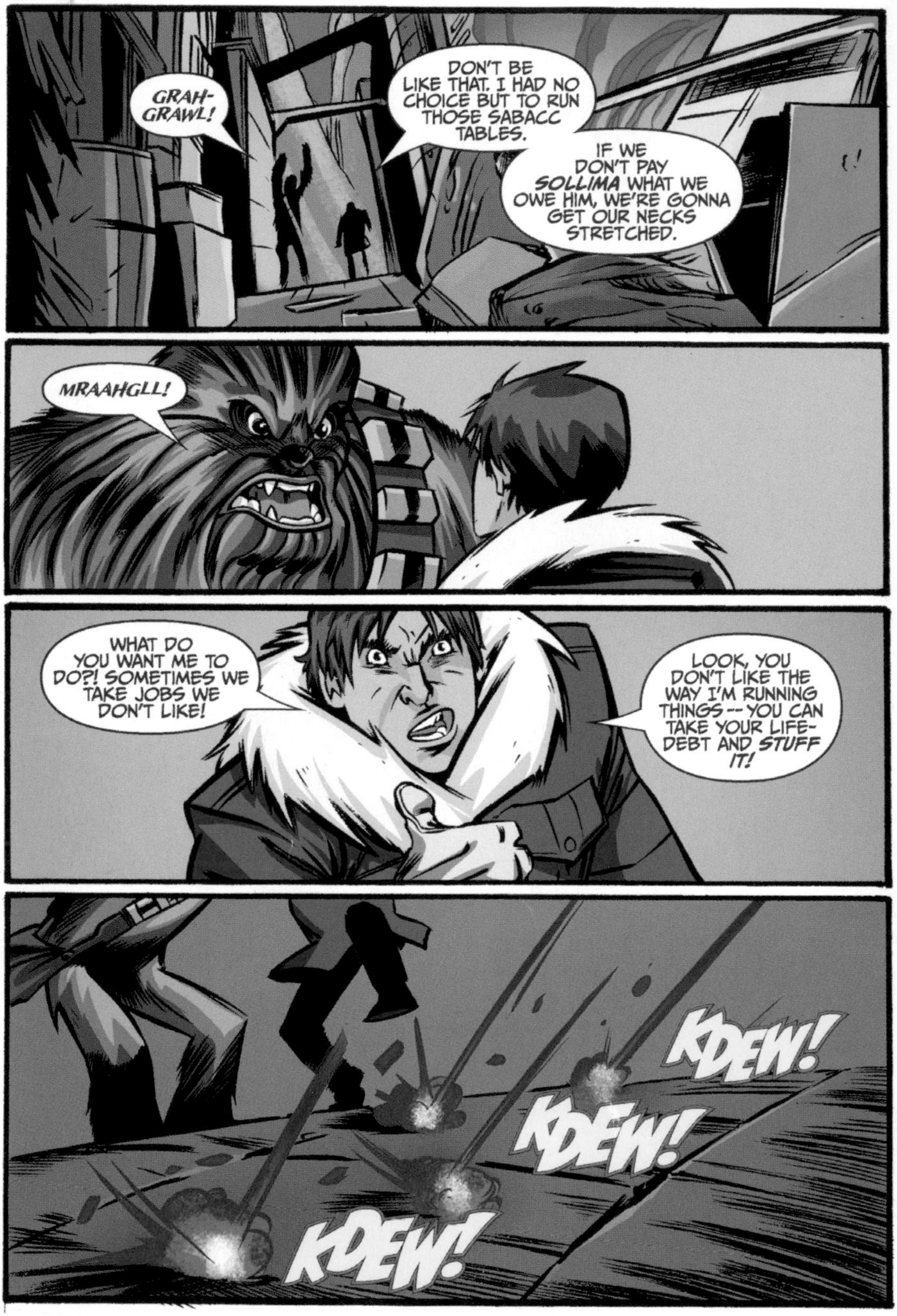
GRAH-GRAWL!
DON'T BE LIKE THAT. I HAD NO CHOICE BUT TO RUN THOSE SABACC TABLES.
IF WE DON'T PAY *SOLLIMA* WHAT WE OWE HIM, WE'RE GONNA GET OUR NECKS STRETCHED.
MRAAHGLL!
WHAT DO YOU WANT ME TO DO?! SOMETIMES WE TAKE JOBS WE DON'T LIKE!
LOOK, YOU DON'T LIKE THE WAY I'M RUNNING THINGS -- YOU CAN TAKE YOUR LIFE-DEBT AND *STUFF IT!*
KDEW!
KDEW!
KDEW!

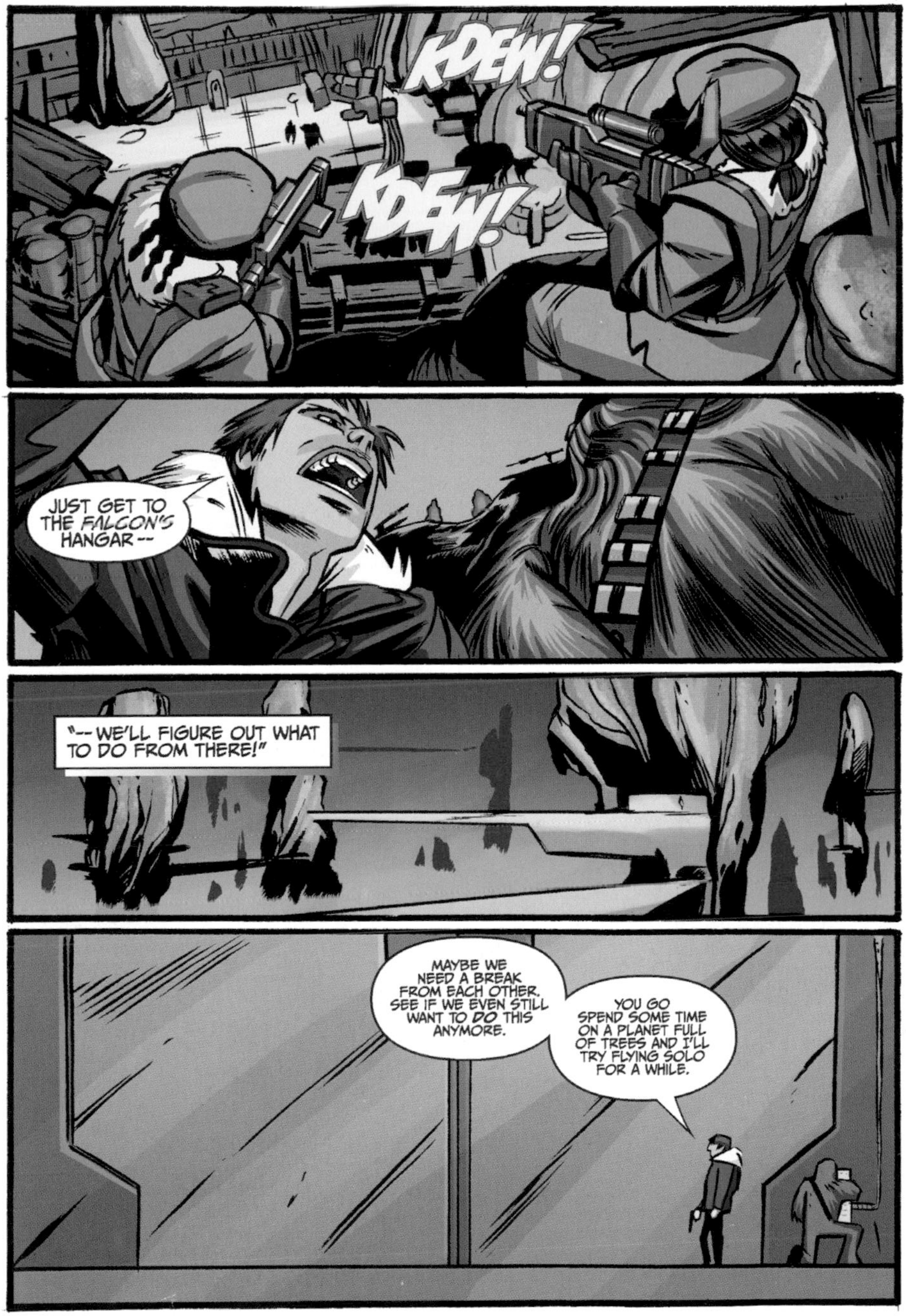
KDEW!
KDEW!
JUST GET TO THE FALCON'S HANGAR --
"-- WE'LL FIGURE OUT WHAT TO DO FROM THERE!"
MAYBE WE NEED A BREAK FROM EACH OTHER. SEE IF WE EVEN STILL WANT TO DO THIS ANYMORE.
YOU GO SPEND SOME TIME ON A PLANET FULL OF TREES AND I'LL TRY FLYING SOLO FOR A WHILE.

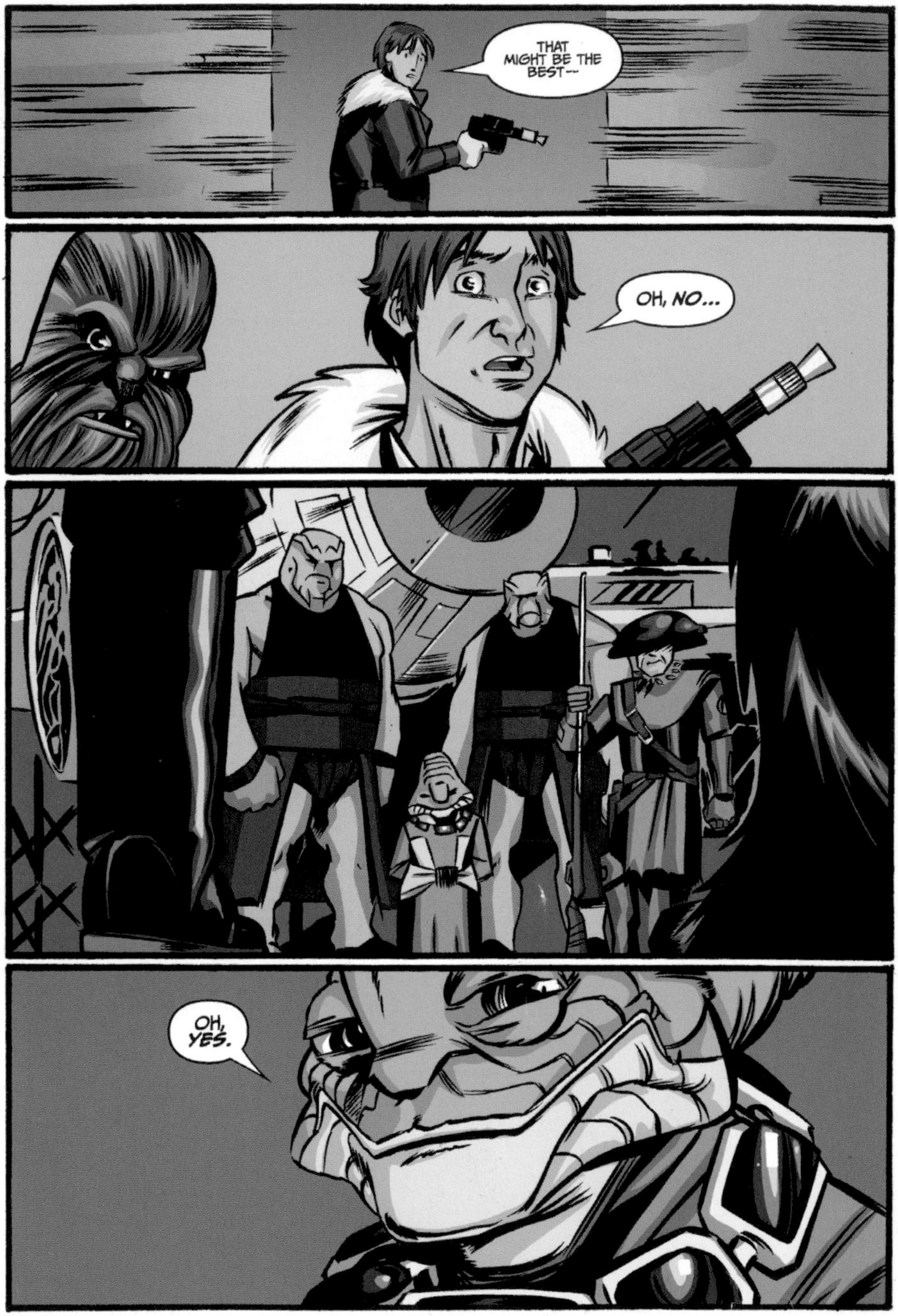
THAT MIGHT BE THE BEST--
OH, NO...
OH, YES.

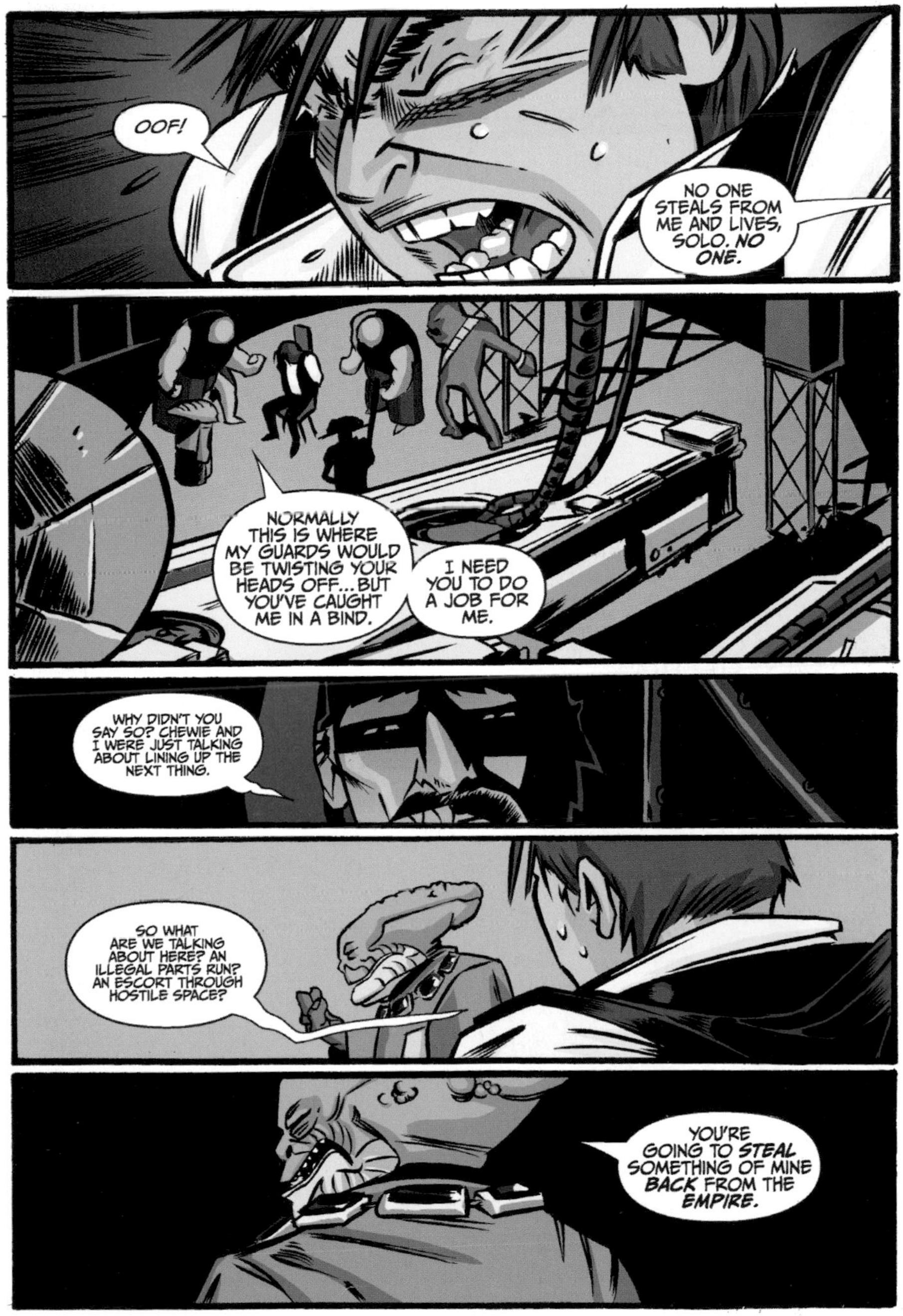
OOF!
NO ONE STEALS FROM ME AND LIVES, SOLO. NO ONE.
NORMALLY THIS IS WHERE MY GUARDS WOULD BE TWISTING YOUR HEADS OFF... BUT YOU'VE CAUGHT ME IN A BIND.
I NEED YOU TO DO A JOB FOR ME.
WHY DIDN'T YOU SAY SO? CHEWIE AND I WERE JUST TALKING ABOUT LINING UP THE NEXT THING.
SO WHAT ARE WE TALKING ABOUT HERE? AN ILLEGAL PARTS RUN? AN ESCORT THROUGH HOSTILE SPACE?
YOU'RE GOING TO STEAL SOMETHING OF MINE BACK FROM THE EMPIRE.

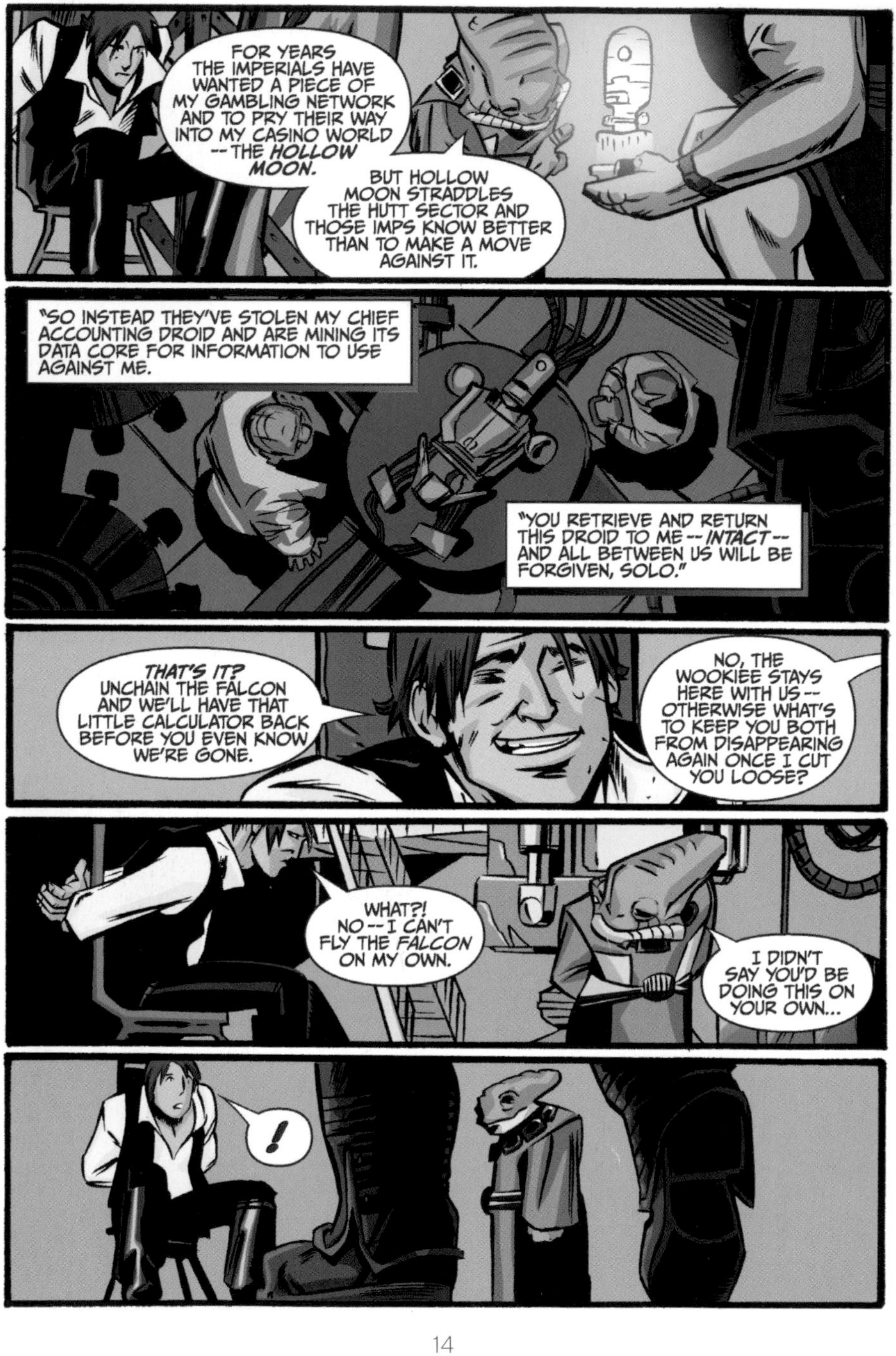
FOR YEARS THE IMPERIALS HAVE WANTED A PIECE OF MY GAMBLING NETWORK AND TO PRY THEIR WAY INTO MY CASINO WORLD --THE *HOLLOW MOON.*
BUT HOLLOW MOON STRADDLES THE HUTT SECTOR AND THOSE IMPS KNOW BETTER THAN TO MAKE A MOVE AGAINST IT.
"SO INSTEAD THEY'VE STOLEN MY CHIEF ACCOUNTING DROID AND ARE MINING ITS DATA CORE FOR INFORMATION TO USE AGAINST ME.
"YOU RETRIEVE AND RETURN THIS DROID TO ME --*INTACT*-- AND ALL BETWEEN US WILL BE FORGIVEN, SOLO."
THAT'S IT? UNCHAIN THE FALCON AND WE'LL HAVE THAT LITTLE CALCULATOR BACK BEFORE YOU EVEN KNOW WE'RE GONE.
NO, THE WOOKIEE STAYS HERE WITH US-- OTHERWISE WHAT'S TO KEEP YOU BOTH FROM DISAPPEARING AGAIN ONCE I CUT YOU LOOSE?
WHAT?! NO--I CAN'T FLY THE *FALCON* ON MY OWN.
I DIDN'T SAY YOU'D BE DOING THIS ON YOUR OWN...
!

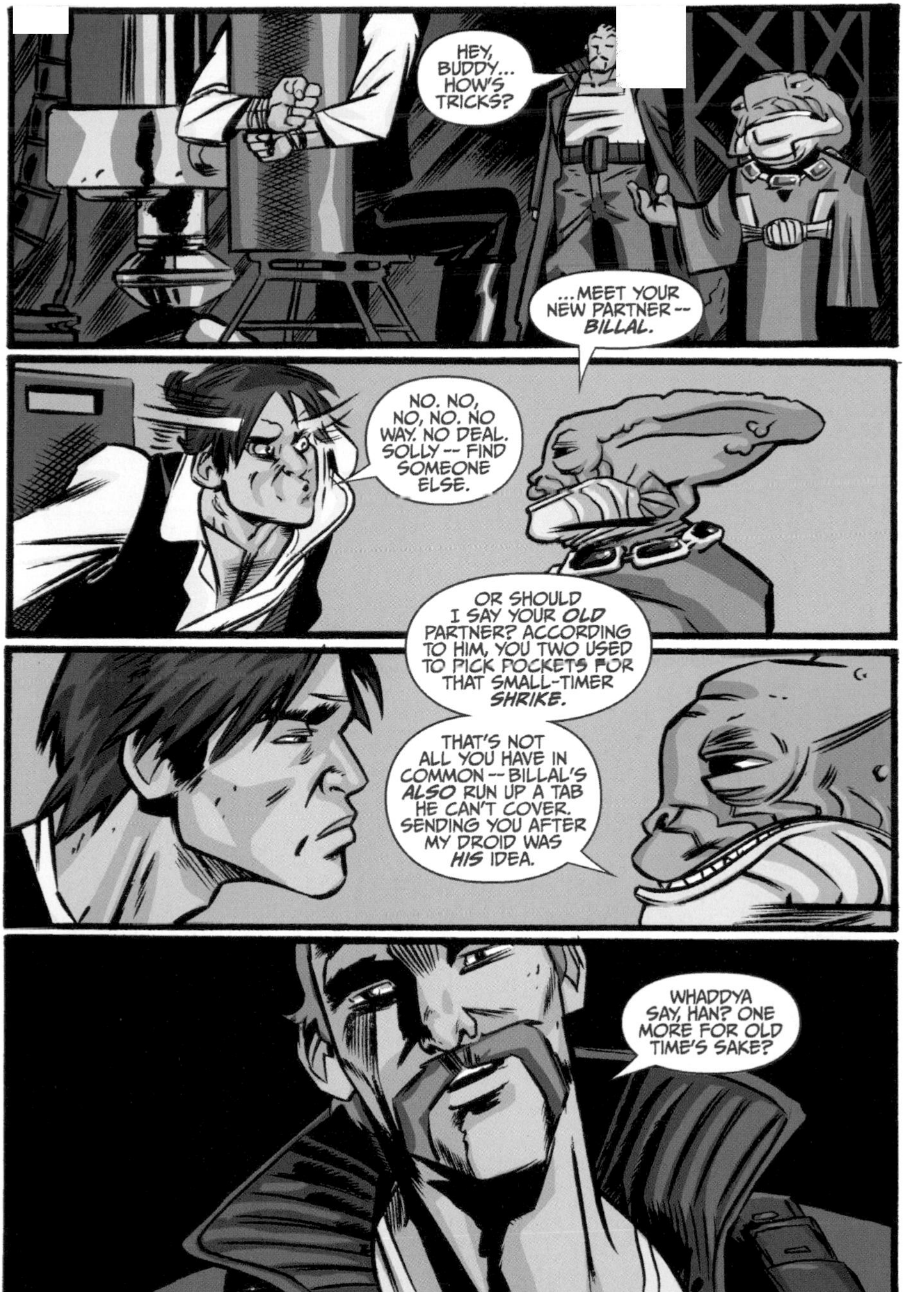
HEY, BUDDY... HOW'S TRICKS?
...MEET YOUR NEW PARTNER -- BILLAL.
NO. NO, NO, NO. NO WAY. NO DEAL. SOLLY -- FIND SOMEONE ELSE.
OR SHOULD I SAY YOUR OLD PARTNER? ACCORDING TO HIM, YOU TWO USED TO PICK POCKETS FOR THAT SMALL-TIMER SHRIKE.
THAT'S NOT ALL YOU HAVE IN COMMON -- BILLAL'S ALSO RUN UP A TAB HE CAN'T COVER. SENDING YOU AFTER MY DROID WAS HIS IDEA.
WHADDYA SAY, HAN? ONE MORE FOR OLD TIME'S SAKE?

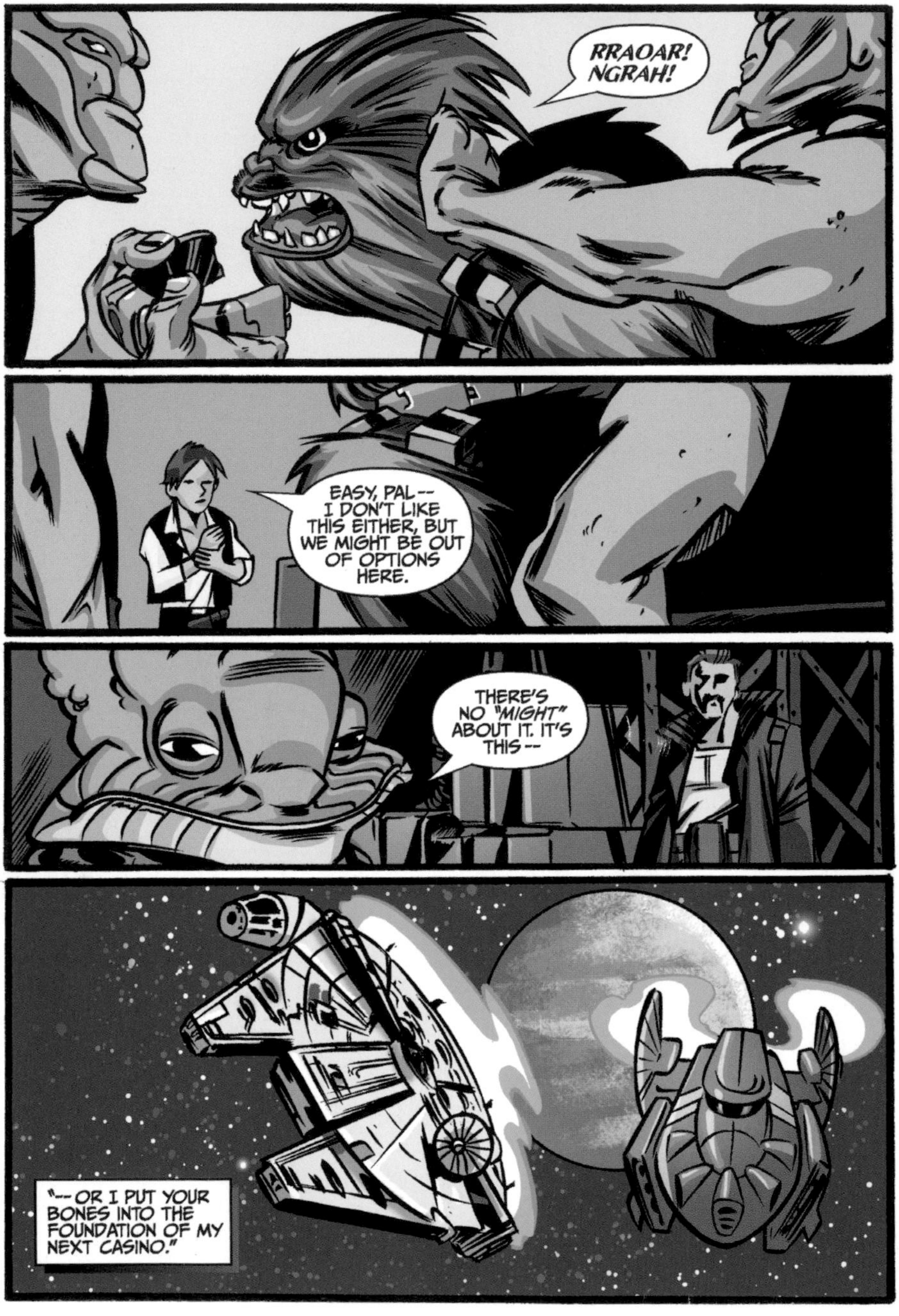
RRAOAR! NGRAH!
EASY, PAL-- I DON'T LIKE THIS EITHER, BUT WE MIGHT BE OUT OF OPTIONS HERE.
THERE'S NO "MIGHT" ABOUT IT. IT'S THIS --
"--OR I PUT YOUR BONES INTO THE FOUNDATION OF MY NEXT CASINO."

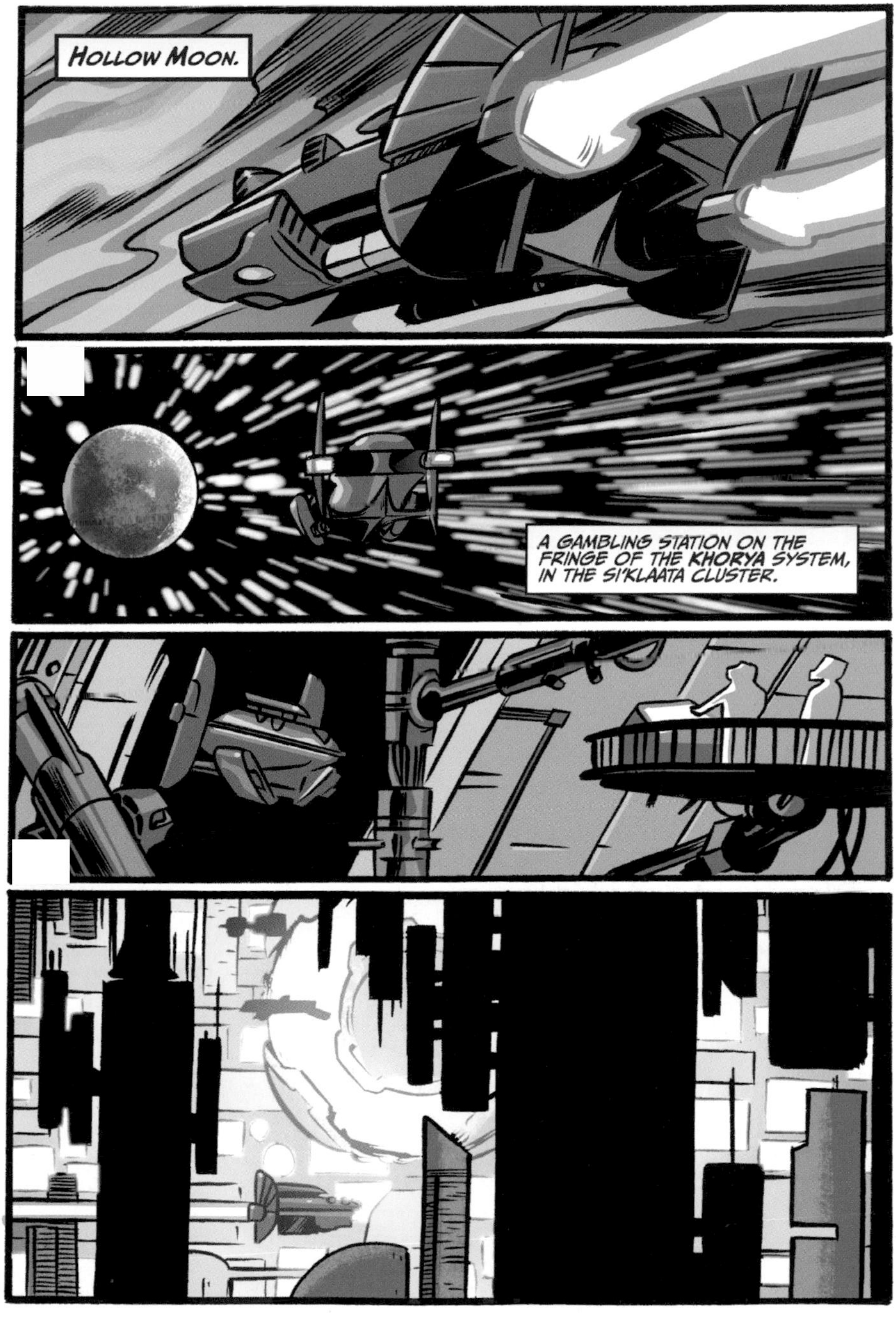
HOLLOW MOON.
A GAMBLING STATION ON THE FRINGE OF THE KHORYA SYSTEM, IN THE SI'KLAATA CLUSTER.

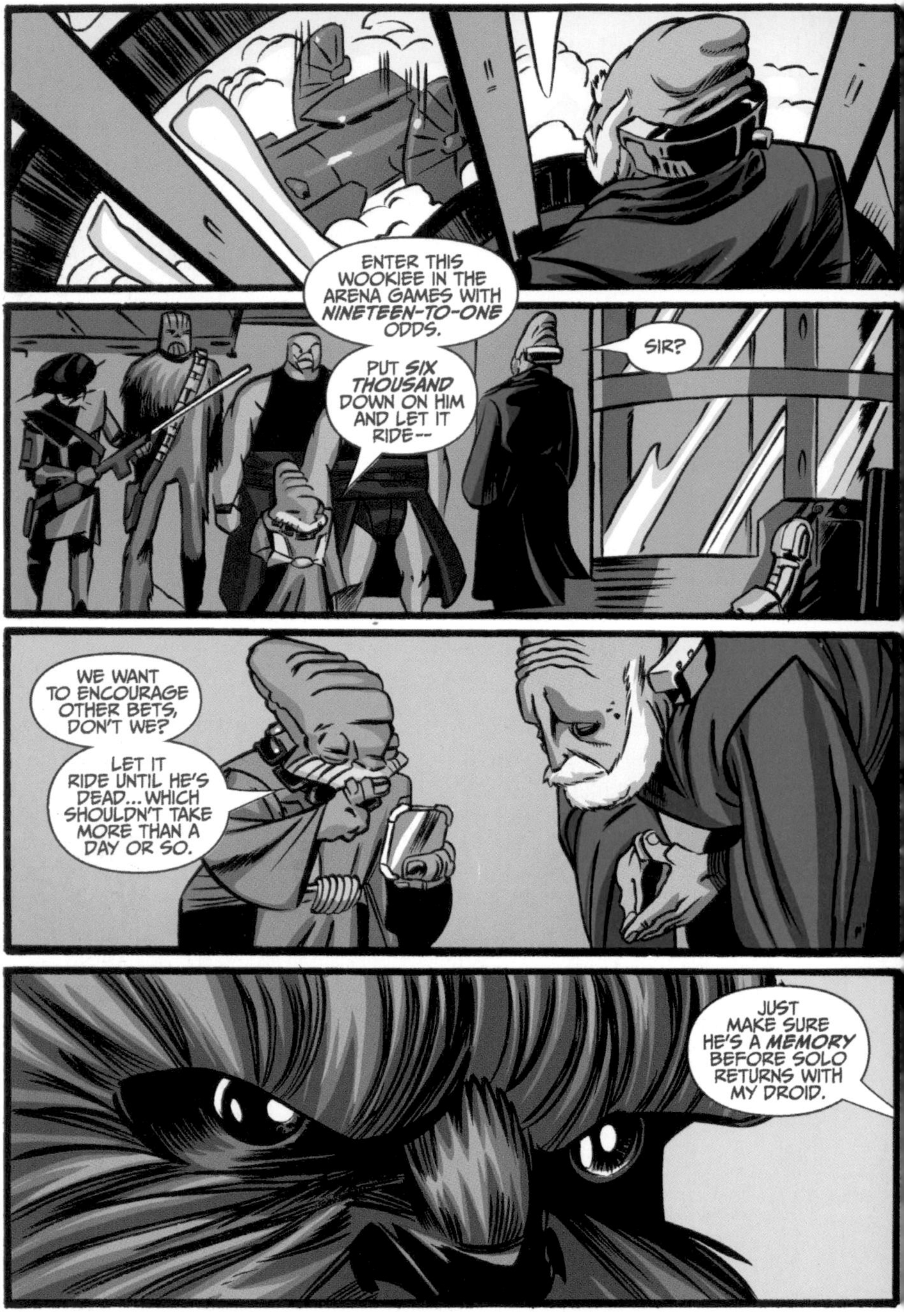
ENTER THIS WOOKIEE IN THE ARENA GAMES WITH NINETEEN-TO-ONE ODDS.
SIR?
PUT SIX THOUSAND DOWN ON HIM AND LET IT RIDE--
WE WANT TO ENCOURAGE OTHER BETS, DON'T WE?
LET IT RIDE UNTIL HE'S DEAD... WHICH SHOULDN'T TAKE MORE THAN A DAY OR SO.
JUST MAKE SURE HE'S A MEMORY BEFORE SOLO RETURNS WITH MY DROID.

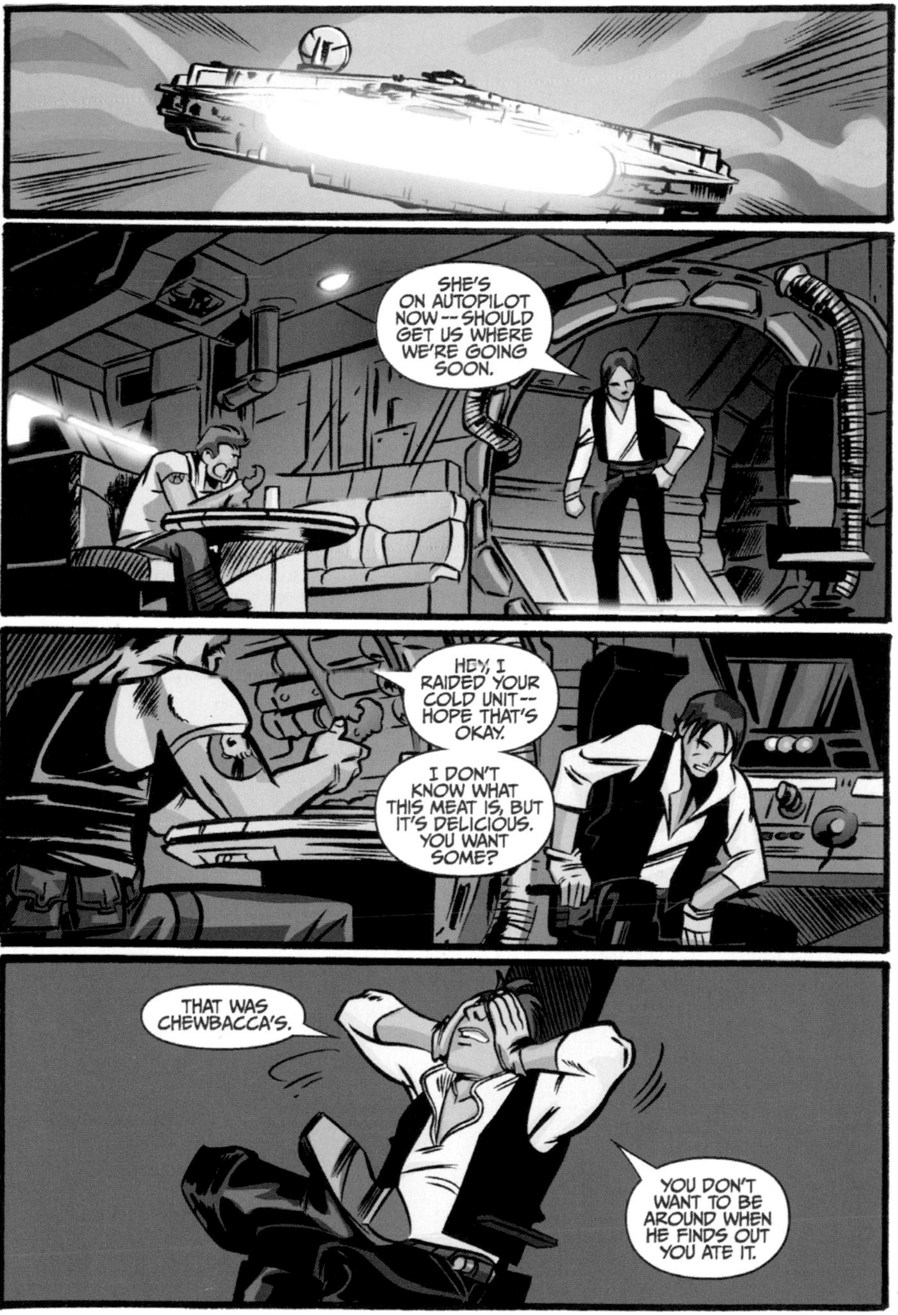
SHE'S ON AUTOPILOT NOW--SHOULD GET US WHERE WE'RE GOING SOON.
HEY, I RAIDED YOUR COLD UNIT--HOPE THAT'S OKAY.
I DON'T KNOW WHAT THIS MEAT IS, BUT IT'S DELICIOUS. YOU WANT SOME?
THAT WAS CHEWBACCA'S.
YOU DON'T WANT TO BE AROUND WHEN HE FINDS OUT YOU ATE IT.

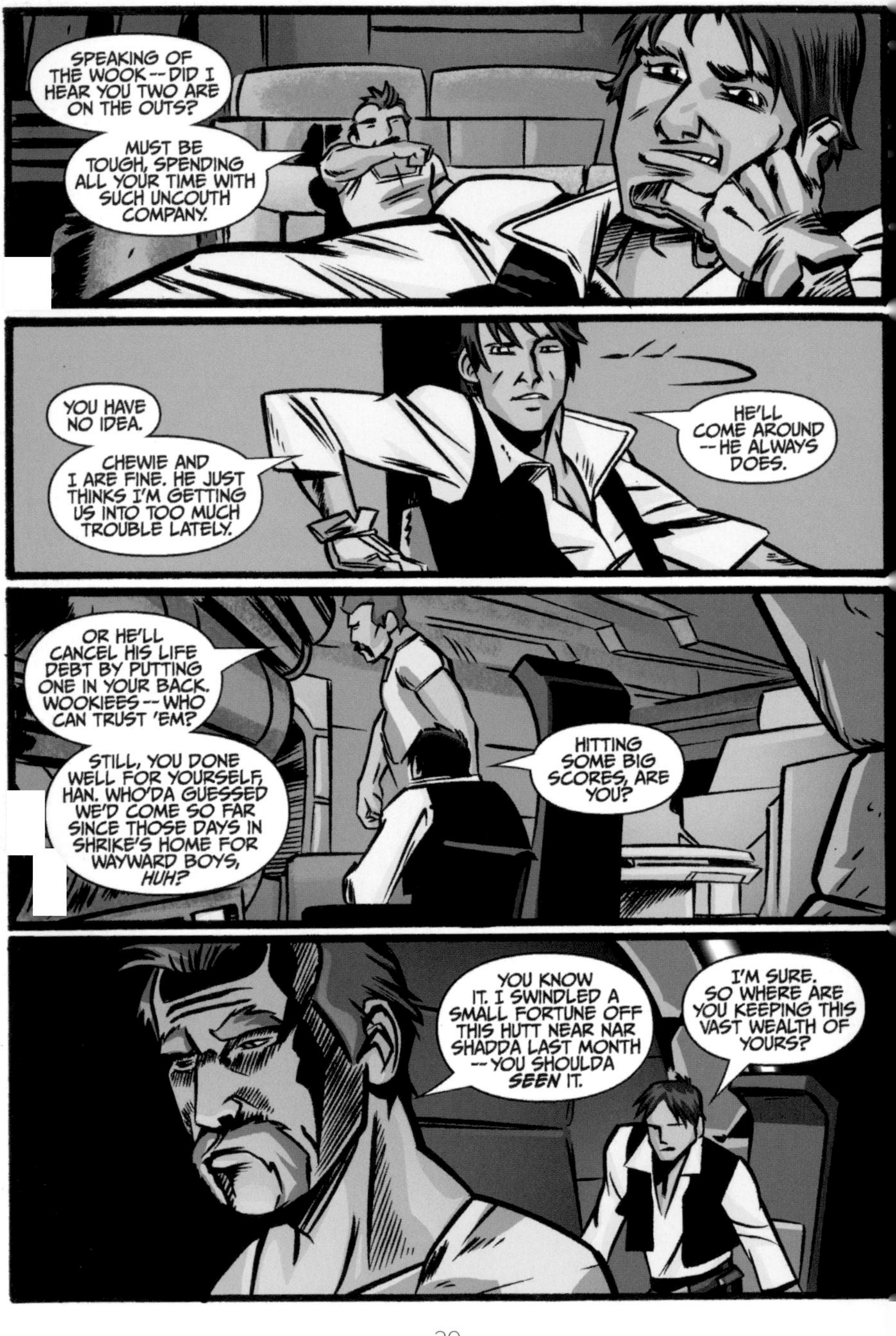
SPEAKING OF THE WOOK--DID I HEAR YOU TWO ARE ON THE OUTS?
MUST BE TOUGH, SPENDING ALL YOUR TIME WITH SUCH UNCOUTH COMPANY.
YOU HAVE NO IDEA.
CHEWIE AND I ARE FINE. HE JUST THINKS I'M GETTING US INTO TOO MUCH TROUBLE LATELY.
HE'LL COME AROUND --HE ALWAYS DOES.
OR HE'LL CANCEL HIS LIFE DEBT BY PUTTING ONE IN YOUR BACK. WOOKIEES--WHO CAN TRUST 'EM?
STILL, YOU DONE WELL FOR YOURSELF, HAN. WHO'DA GUESSED WE'D COME SO FAR SINCE THOSE DAYS IN SHRIKE'S HOME FOR WAYWARD BOYS, *HUH?*
HITTING SOME BIG SCORES, ARE YOU?
YOU KNOW IT. I SWINDLED A SMALL FORTUNE OFF THIS HUTT NEAR NAR SHADDA LAST MONTH --YOU SHOULDA *SEEN* IT.
I'M SURE. SO WHERE ARE YOU KEEPING THIS VAST WEALTH OF YOURS?

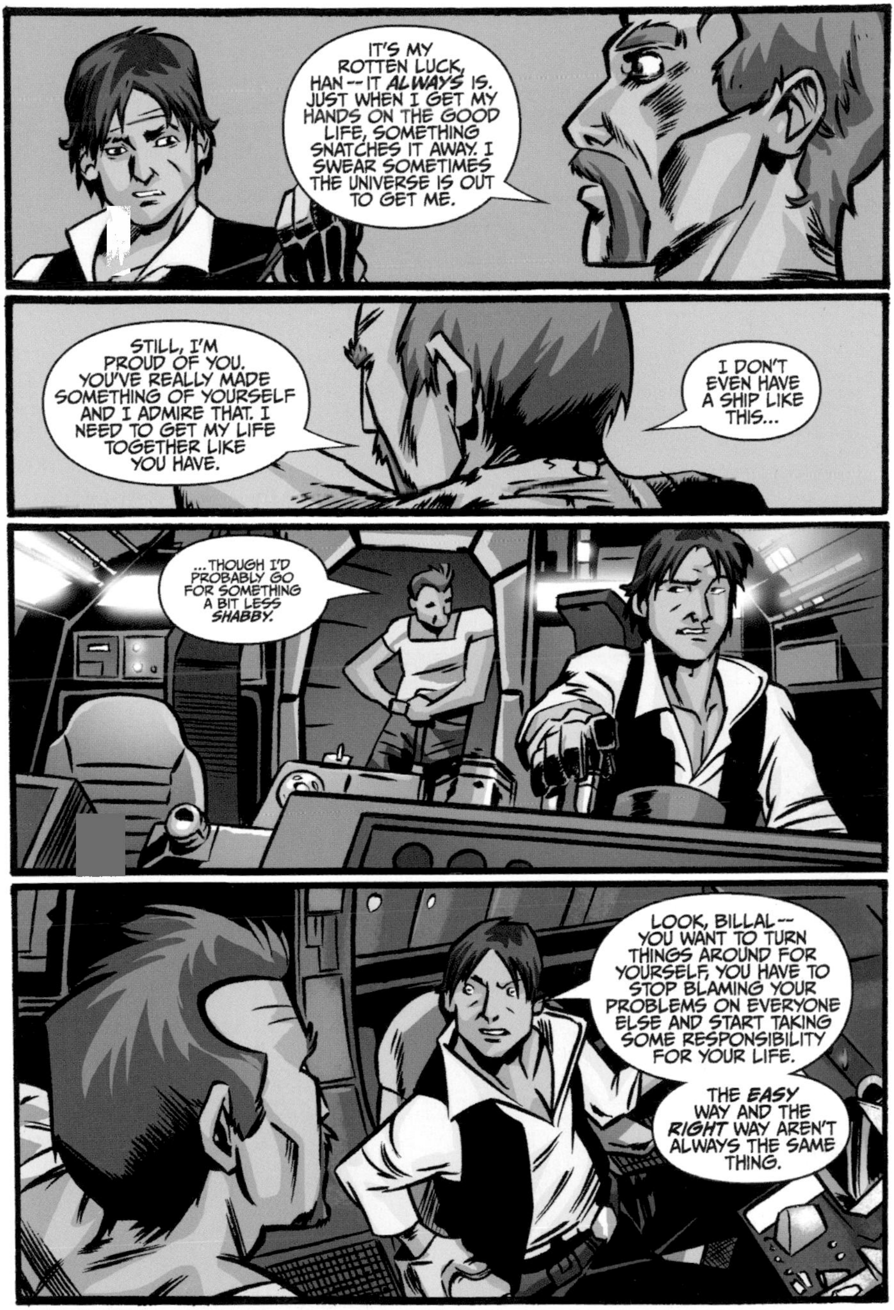

IT'S MY ROTTEN LUCK, HAN--IT *ALWAYS* IS. JUST WHEN I GET MY HANDS ON THE GOOD LIFE, SOMETHING SNATCHES IT AWAY. I SWEAR SOMETIMES THE UNIVERSE IS OUT TO GET ME.
STILL, I'M PROUD OF YOU. YOU'VE REALLY MADE SOMETHING OF YOURSELF AND I ADMIRE THAT. I NEED TO GET MY LIFE TOGETHER LIKE YOU HAVE.
I DON'T EVEN HAVE A SHIP LIKE THIS...
...THOUGH I'D PROBABLY GO FOR SOMETHING A BIT LESS *SHABBY.*
LOOK, BILLAL--YOU WANT TO TURN THINGS AROUND FOR YOURSELF, YOU HAVE TO STOP BLAMING YOUR PROBLEMS ON EVERYONE ELSE AND START TAKING SOME RESPONSIBILITY FOR YOUR LIFE.
THE *EASY* WAY AND THE *RIGHT* WAY AREN'T ALWAYS THE SAME THING.

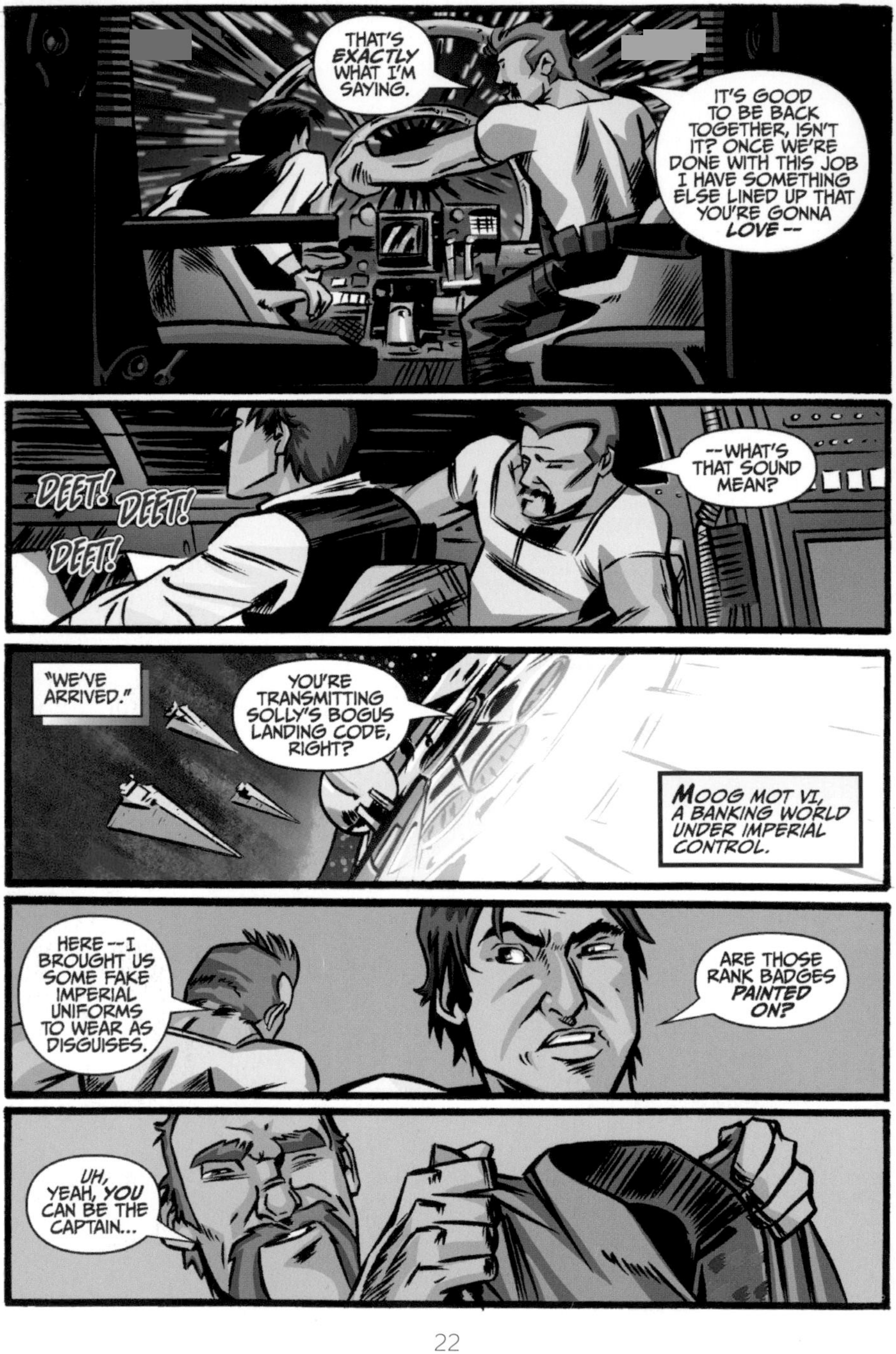
THAT'S *EXACTLY* WHAT I'M SAYING.
IT'S GOOD TO BE BACK TOGETHER, ISN'T IT? ONCE WE'RE DONE WITH THIS JOB I HAVE SOMETHING ELSE LINED UP THAT YOU'RE GONNA *LOVE* --
DEET! DEET! DEET!
--WHAT'S THAT SOUND MEAN?
"WE'VE ARRIVED."
YOU'RE TRANSMITTING SOLLY'S BOGUS LANDING CODE, RIGHT?
MOOG MOT VI, A BANKING WORLD UNDER IMPERIAL CONTROL.
HERE--I BROUGHT US SOME FAKE IMPERIAL UNIFORMS TO WEAR AS DISGUISES.
ARE THOSE RANK BADGES *PAINTED* *ON?*
UH, YEAH, *YOU* CAN BE THE CAPTAIN...

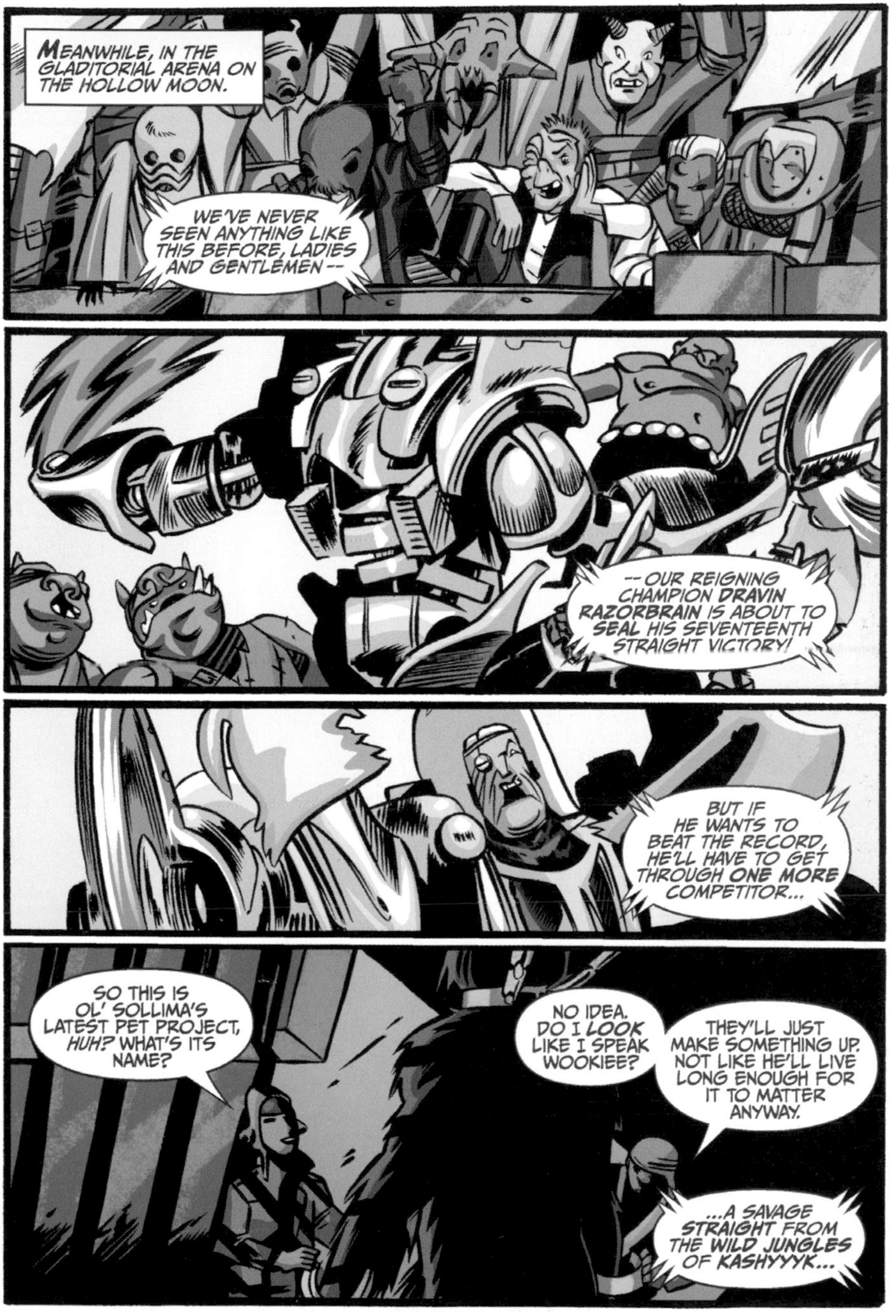
MEANWHILE, IN THE GLADITORIAL ARENA ON THE HOLLOW MOON.
WE'VE NEVER SEEN ANYTHING LIKE THIS BEFORE, LADIES AND GENTLEMEN --
-- OUR REIGNING CHAMPION DRAVIN RAZORBRAIN IS ABOUT TO SEAL HIS SEVENTEENTH STRAIGHT VICTORY!
BUT IF HE WANTS TO BEAT THE RECORD, HE'LL HAVE TO GET THROUGH ONE MORE COMPETITOR...
SO THIS IS OL' SOLLIMA'S LATEST PET PROJECT, HUH? WHAT'S ITS NAME?
NO IDEA. DO I LOOK LIKE I SPEAK WOOKIEE?
THEY'LL JUST MAKE SOMETHING UP. NOT LIKE HE'LL LIVE LONG ENOUGH FOR IT TO MATTER ANYWAY.
...A SAVAGE STRAIGHT FROM THE WILD JUNGLES OF KASHYYYK...

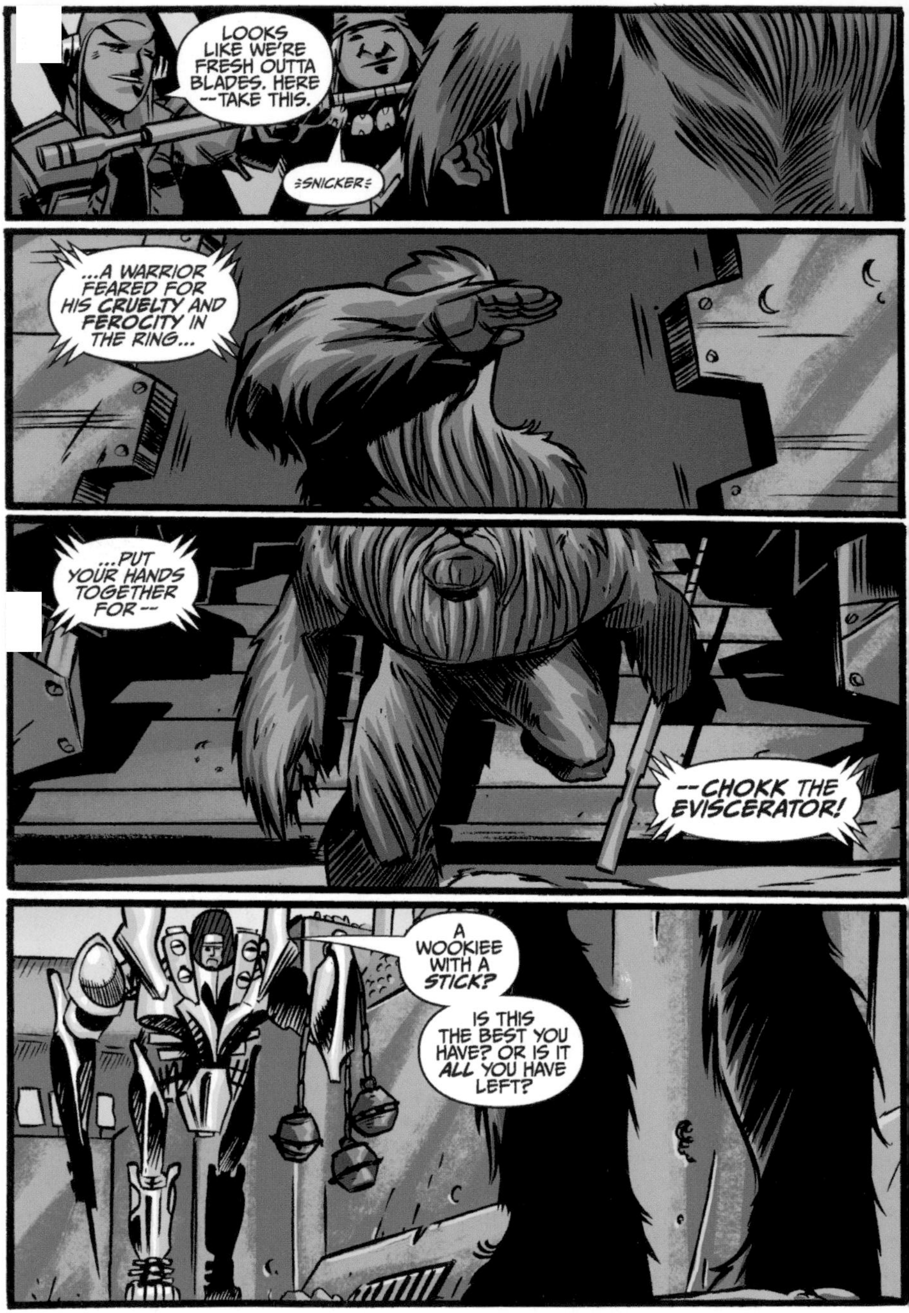
LOOKS LIKE WE'RE FRESH OUTTA BLADES. HERE --TAKE THIS.
SNICKER
...A WARRIOR FEARED FOR HIS CRUELTY AND FEROCITY IN THE RING...
...PUT YOUR HANDS TOGETHER FOR--
--CHOKK THE EVISCERATOR!
A WOOKIEE WITH A STICK?
IS THIS THE BEST YOU HAVE? OR IS IT ALL YOU HAVE LEFT?

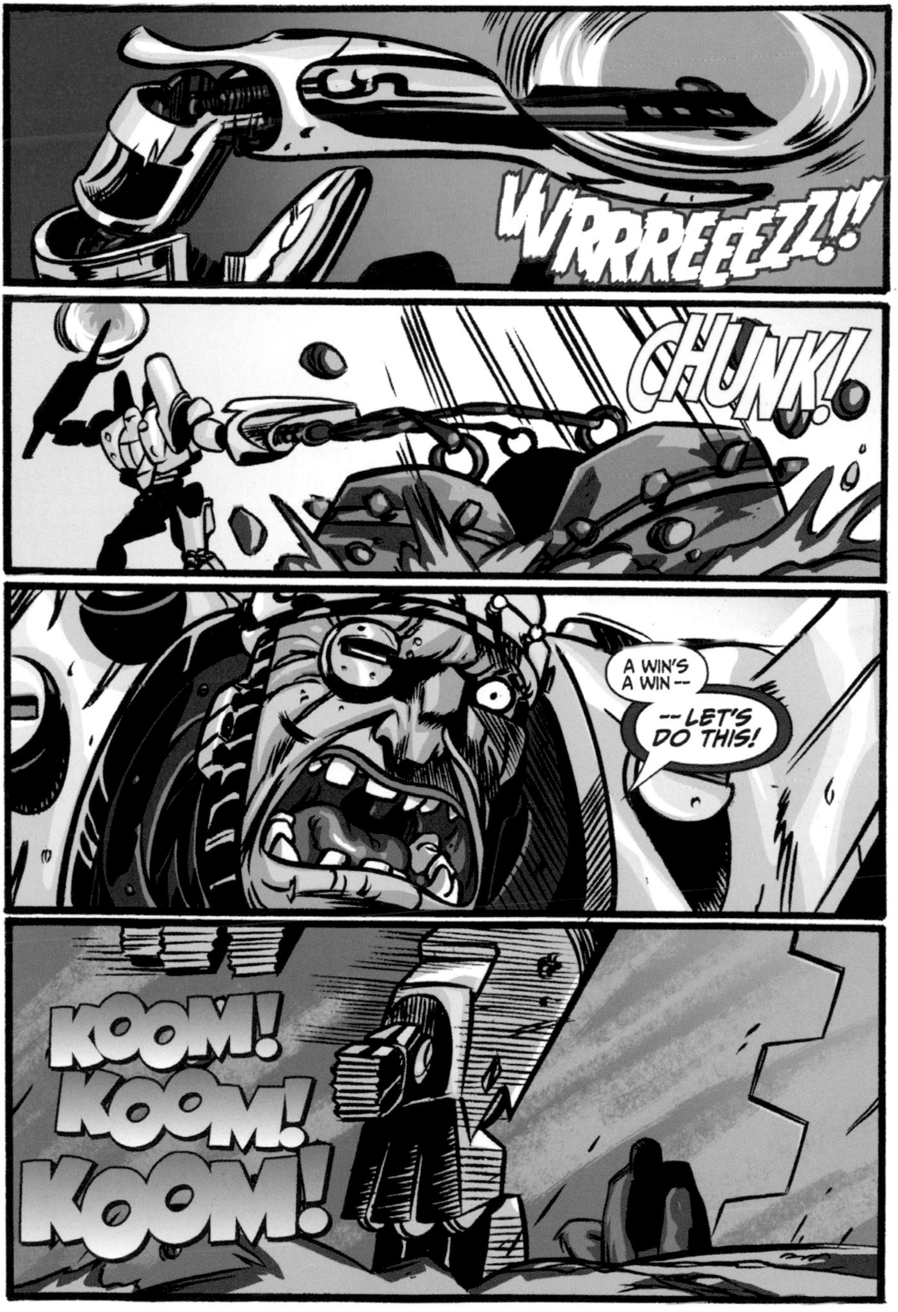
WRRREEEZZ!!
CHUNK!
A WIN'S A WIN --
-- LET'S DO THIS!
KOOM! KOOM! KOOM!

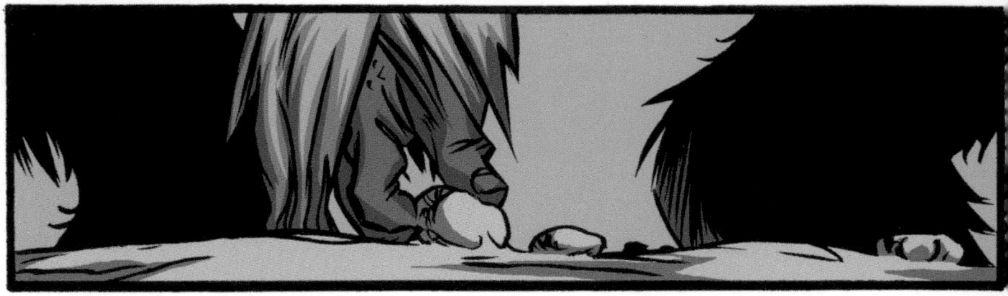
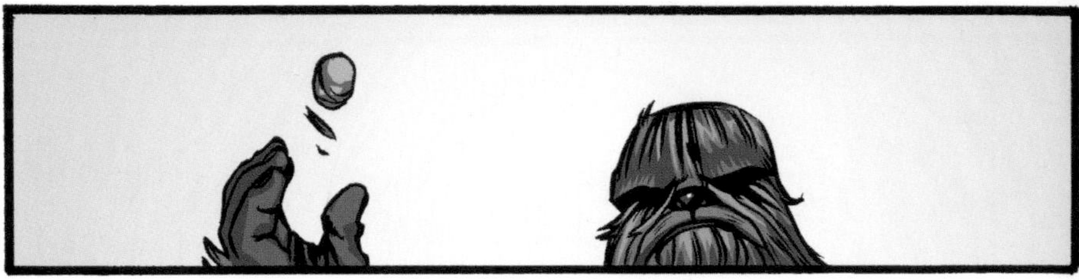
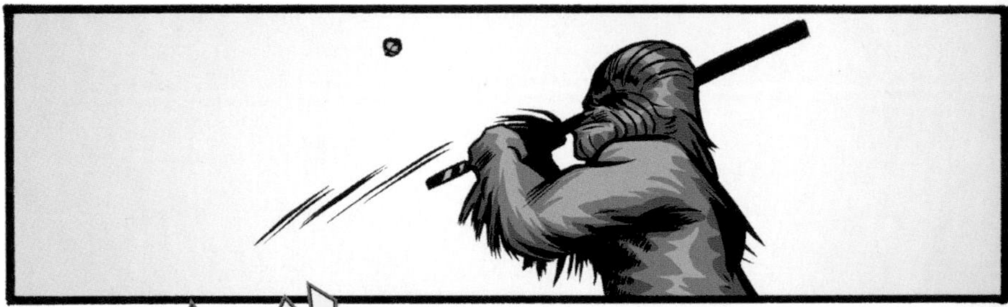
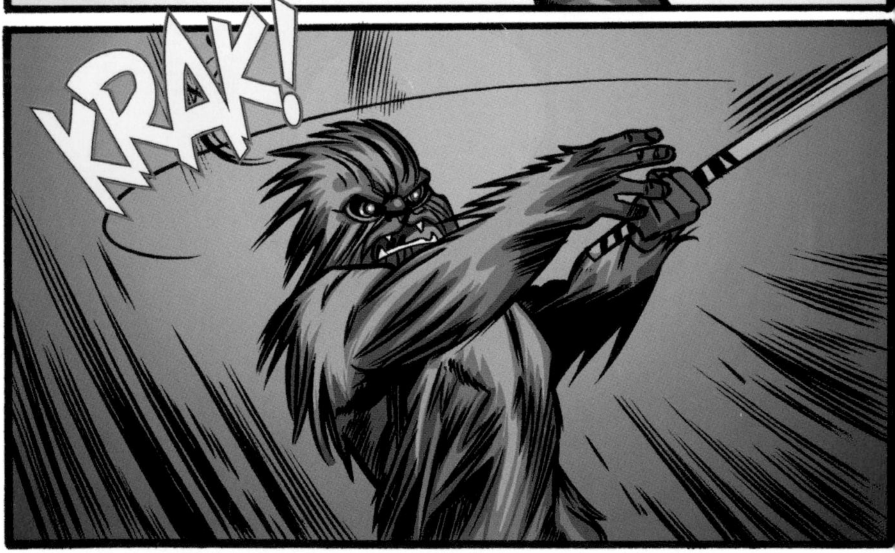
KRAK!

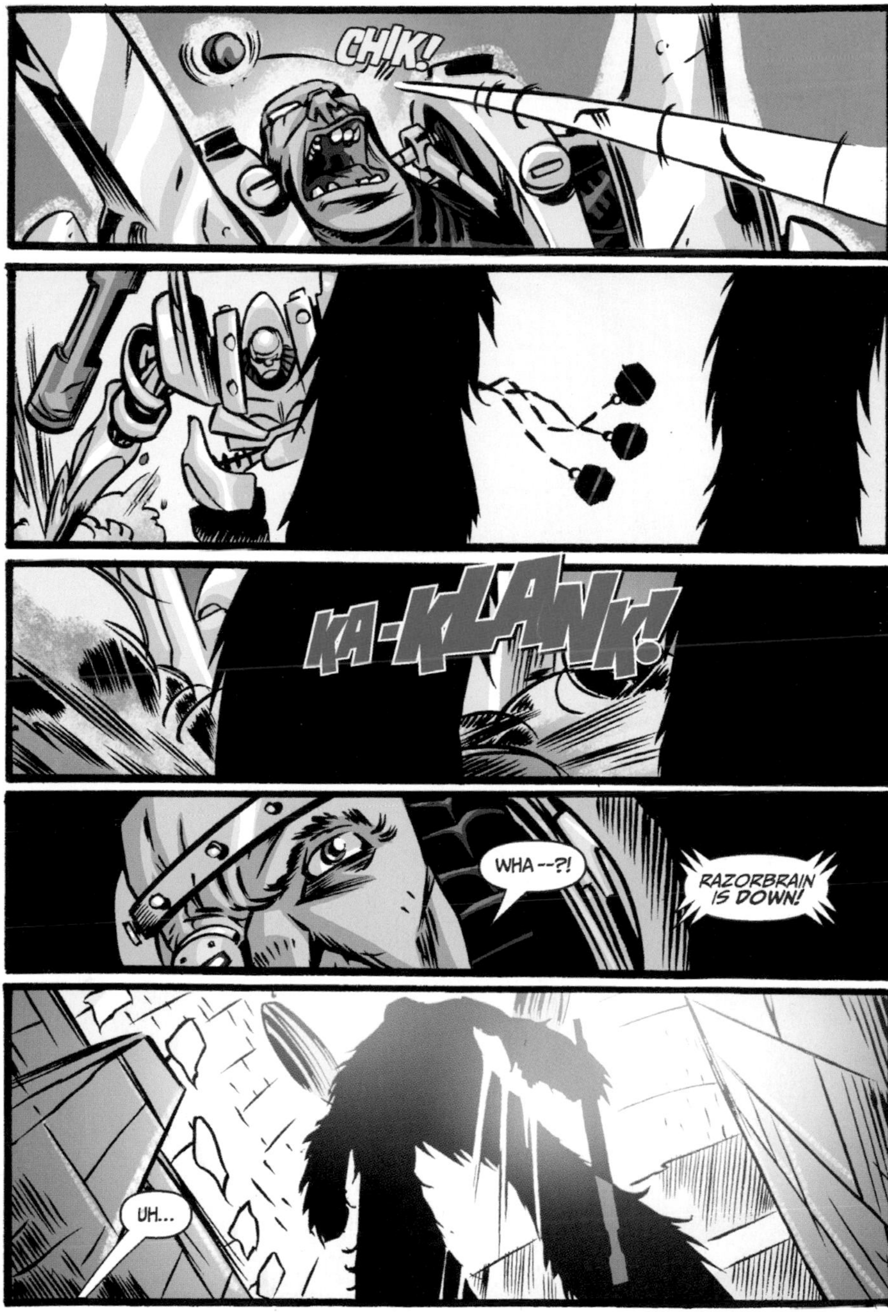
CHIK!
KA-KLANK!
WHA--?!
RAZORBRAIN IS DOWN!
UH...

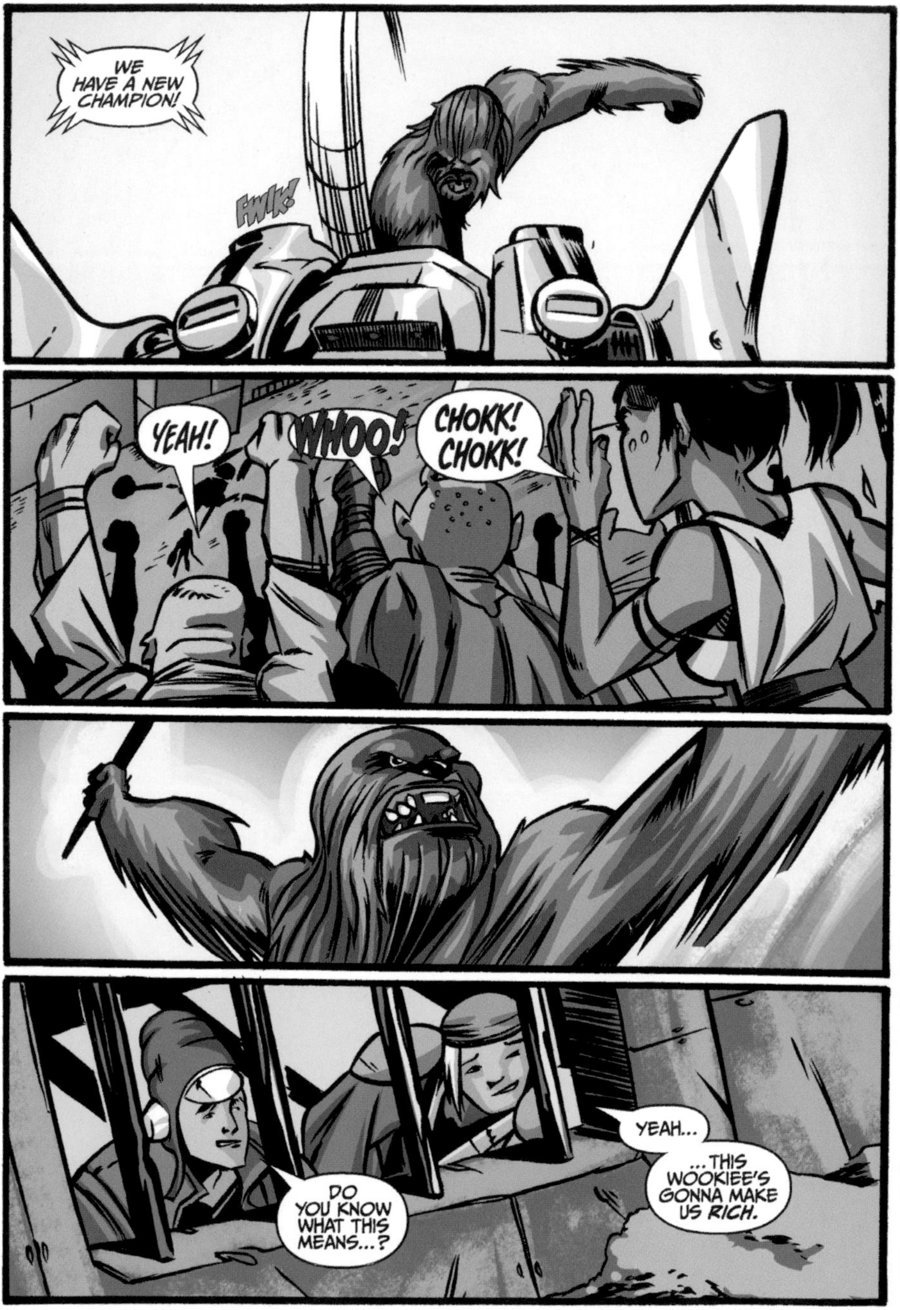
WE HAVE A NEW CHAMPION!
FWIK!
YEAH!
WHOO!
CHOKK! CHOKK!
DO YOU KNOW WHAT THIS MEANS...?
YEAH...
...THIS WOOKIEE'S GONNA MAKE US RICH.

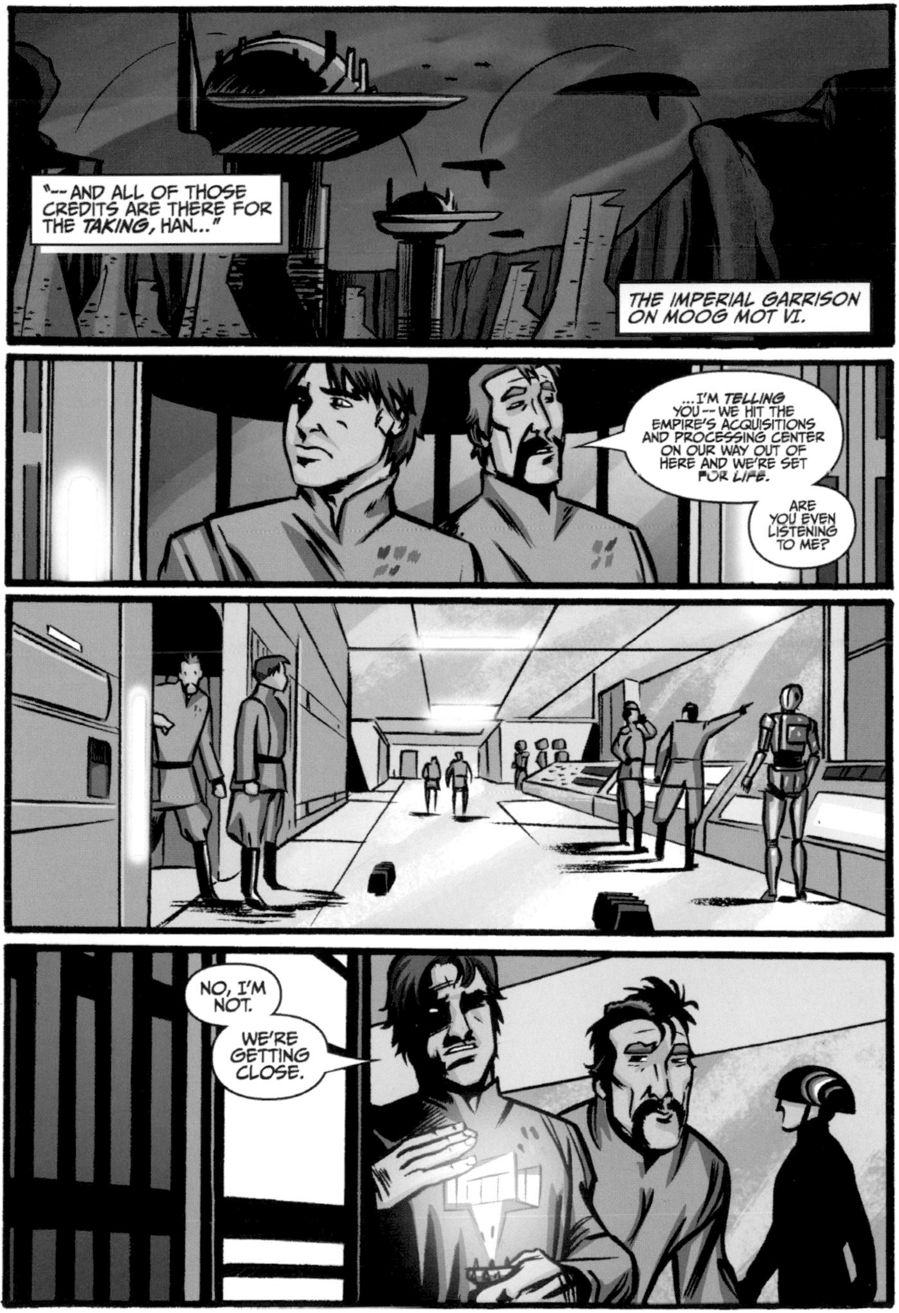
"--AND ALL OF THOSE CREDITS ARE THERE FOR THE *TAKING*, HAN..."
THE IMPERIAL GARRISON ON MOOG MOT VI.
...I'M *TELLING* YOU--WE HIT THE EMPIRE'S ACQUISITIONS AND PROCESSING CENTER ON OUR WAY OUT OF HERE AND WE'RE SET FOR *LIFE*.
ARE YOU EVEN LISTENING TO ME?
NO, I'M NOT.
WE'RE GETTING CLOSE.

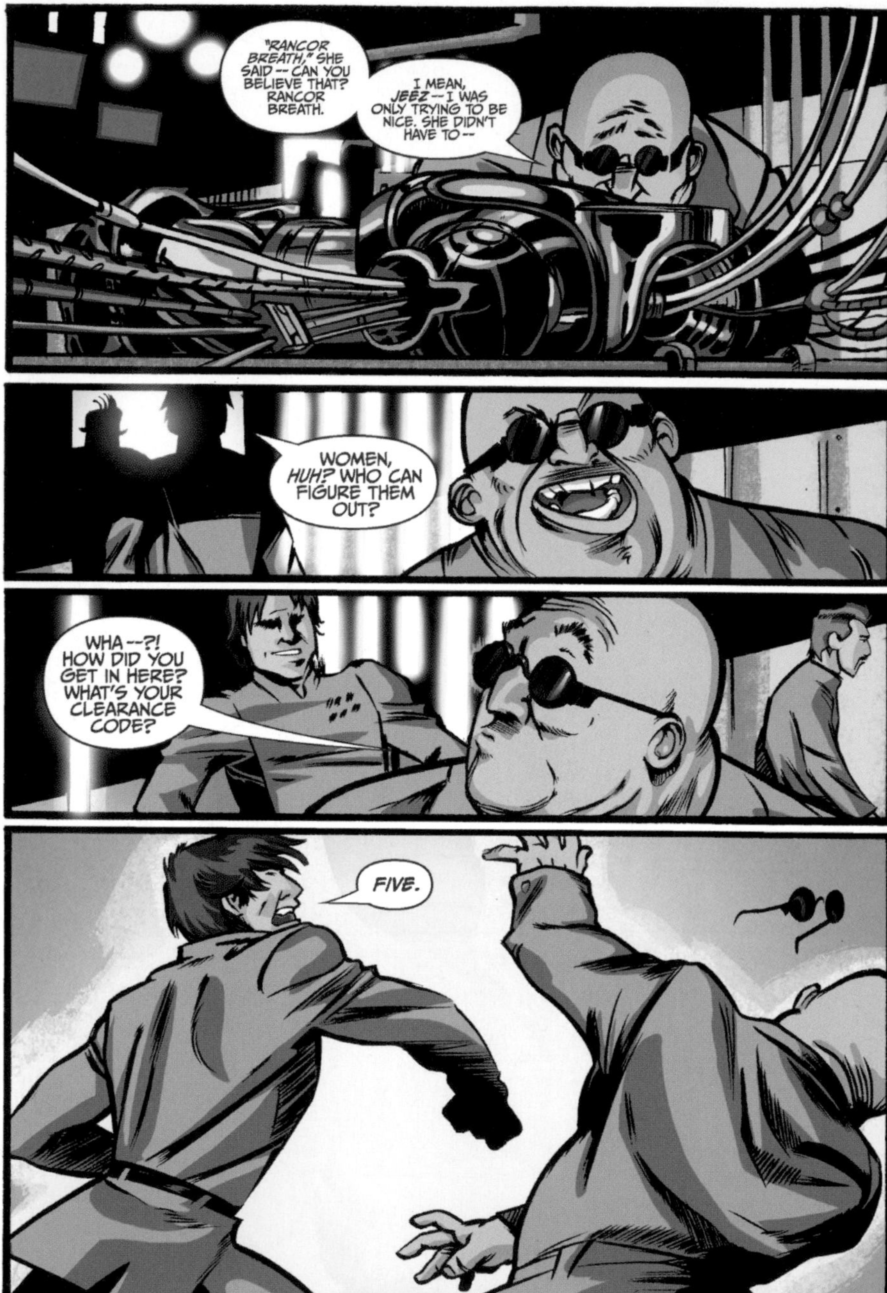
"RANCOR BREATH," SHE SAID -- CAN YOU BELIEVE THAT? RANCOR BREATH.
I MEAN, JEEZ -- I WAS ONLY TRYING TO BE NICE. SHE DIDN'T HAVE TO --
WOMEN, HUH? WHO CAN FIGURE THEM OUT?
WHA --?! HOW DID YOU GET IN HERE? WHAT'S YOUR CLEARANCE CODE?
FIVE.

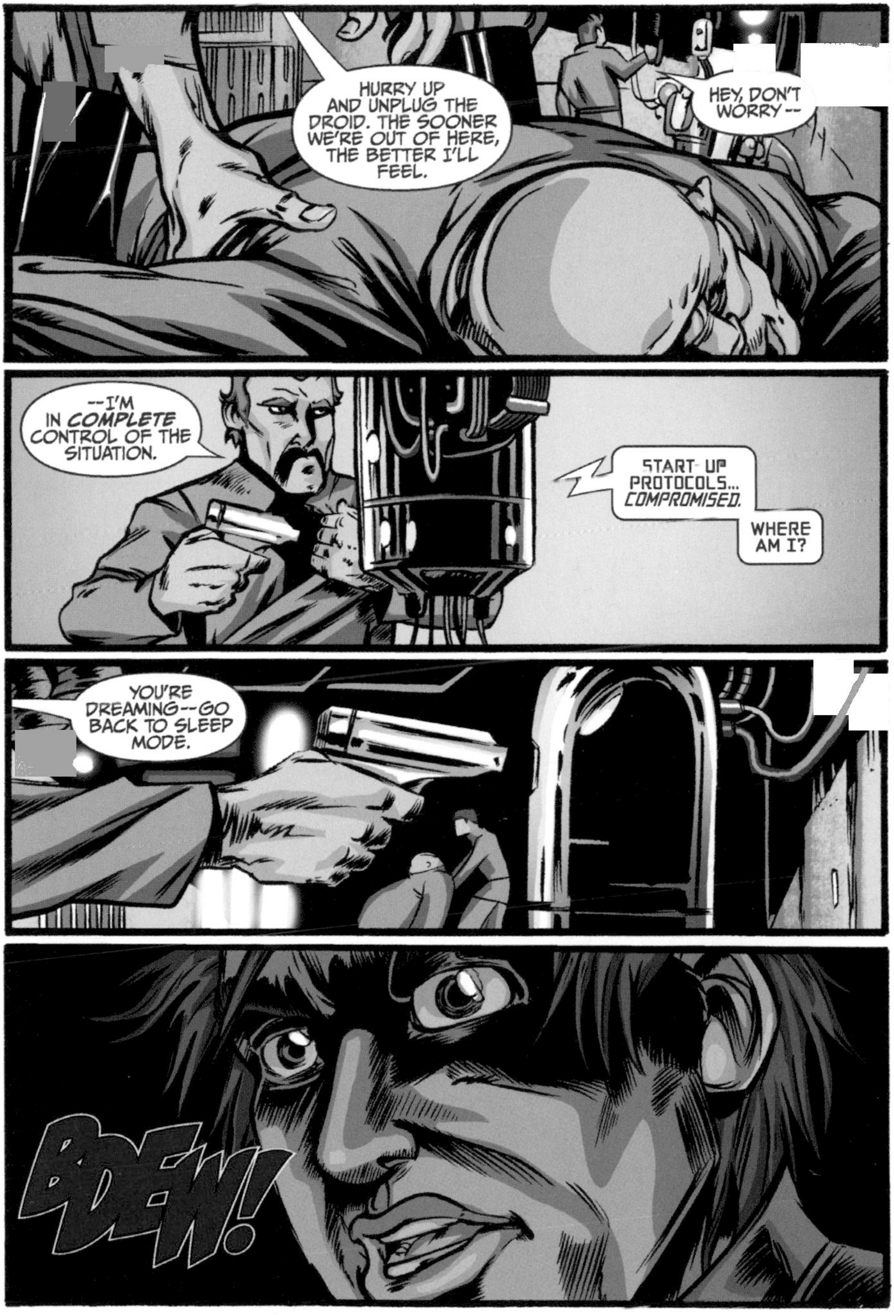
HURRY UP AND UNPLUG THE DROID. THE SOONER WE'RE OUT OF HERE, THE BETTER I'LL FEEL.
HEY, DON'T WORRY--
--I'M IN *COMPLETE* CONTROL OF THE SITUATION.
START-UP PROTOCOLS... *COMPROMISED.*
WHERE AM I?
YOU'RE DREAMING--GO BACK TO SLEEP MODE.
BDEW!

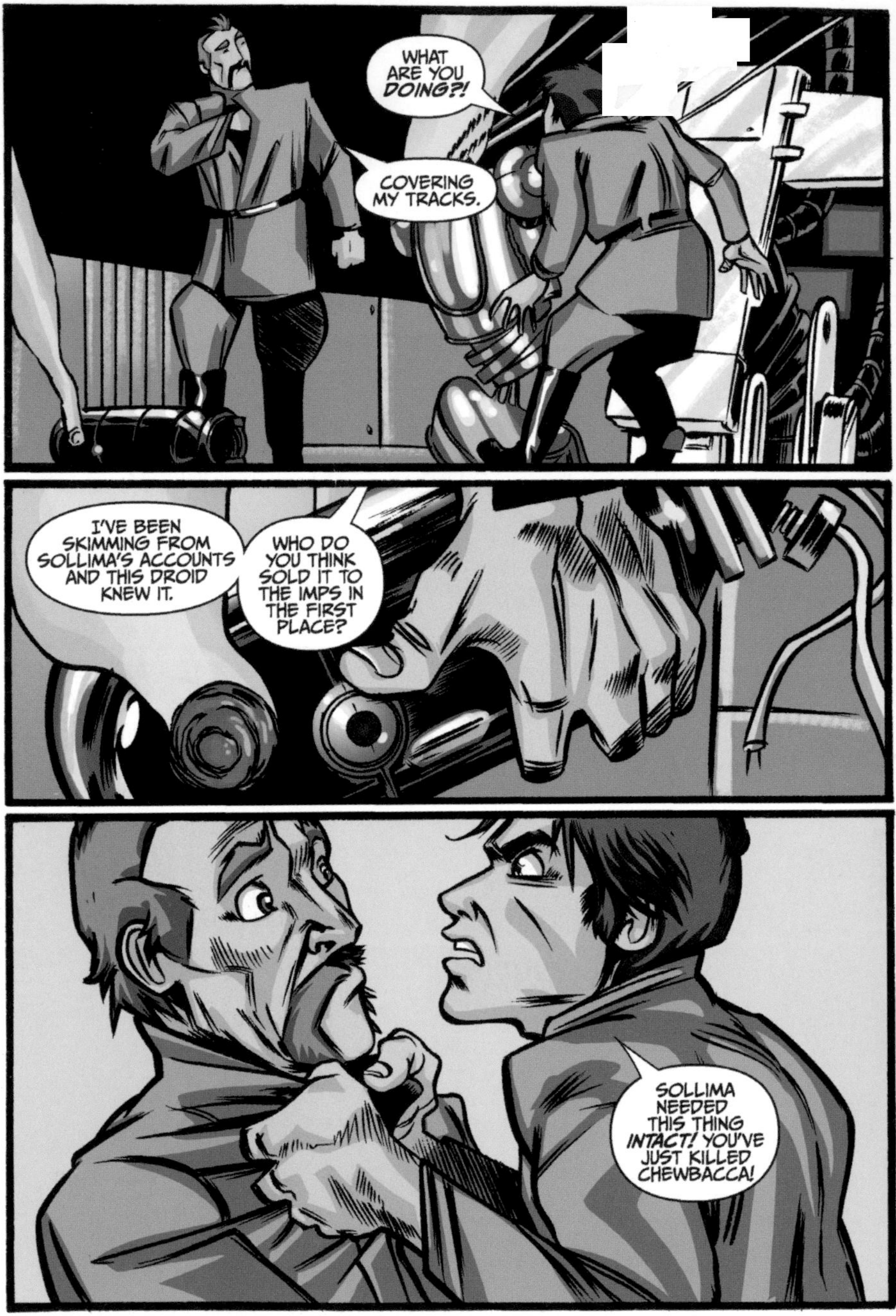
WHAT ARE YOU DOING?!
COVERING MY TRACKS.
I'VE BEEN SKIMMING FROM SOLLIMA'S ACCOUNTS AND THIS DROID KNEW IT.
WHO DO YOU THINK SOLD IT TO THE IMPS IN THE FIRST PLACE?
SOLLIMA NEEDED THIS THING INTACT! YOU'VE JUST KILLED CHEWBACCA!

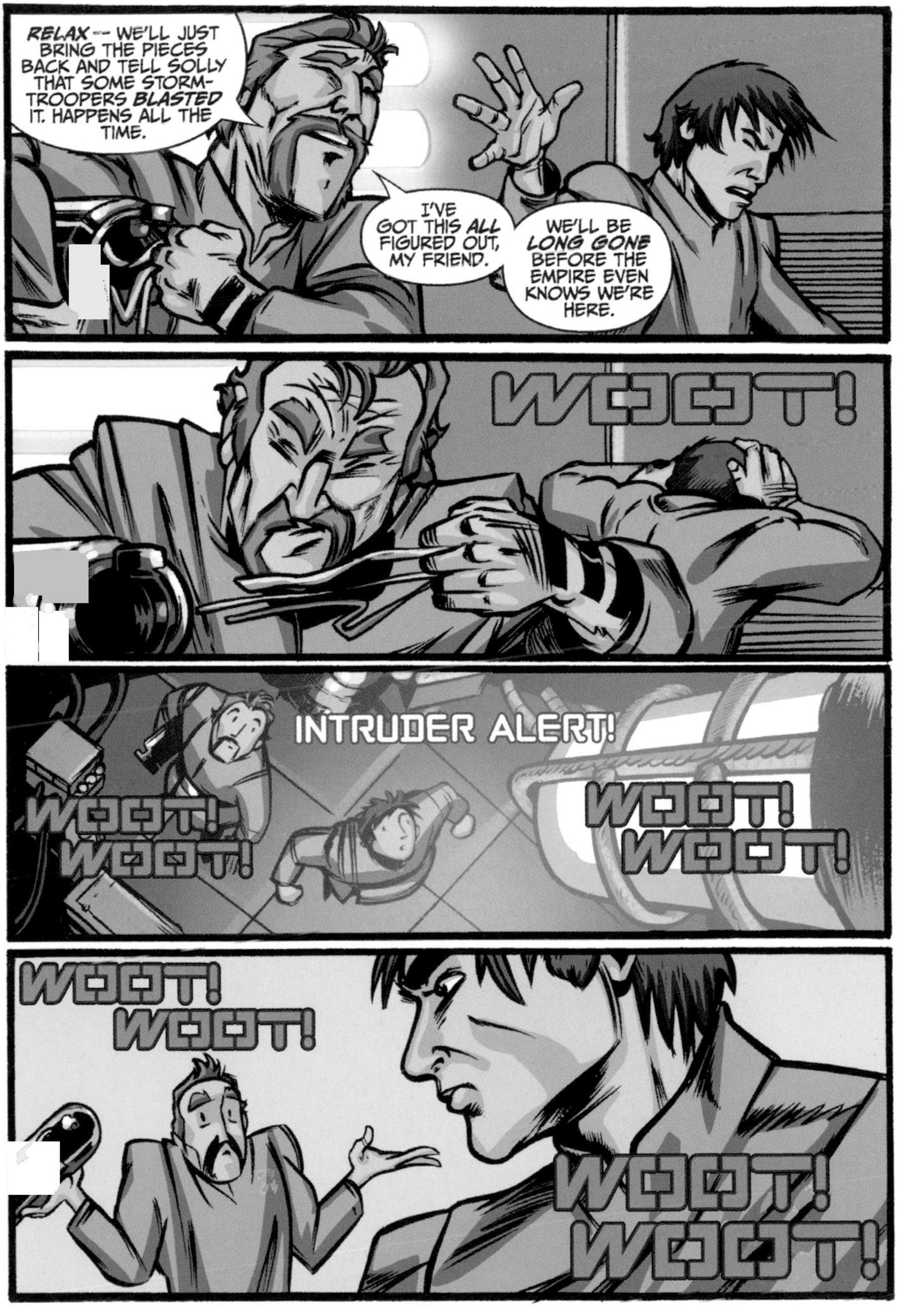
RELAX -- WE'LL JUST BRING THE PIECES BACK AND TELL SOLLY THAT SOME STORM-TROOPERS BLASTED IT. HAPPENS ALL THE TIME.
I'VE GOT THIS ALL FIGURED OUT, MY FRIEND.
WE'LL BE LONG GONE BEFORE THE EMPIRE EVEN KNOWS WE'RE HERE.
WOOT!
INTRUDER ALERT!
WOOT! WOOT!
WOOT! WOOT!
WOOT! WOOT!
WOOT! WOOT!

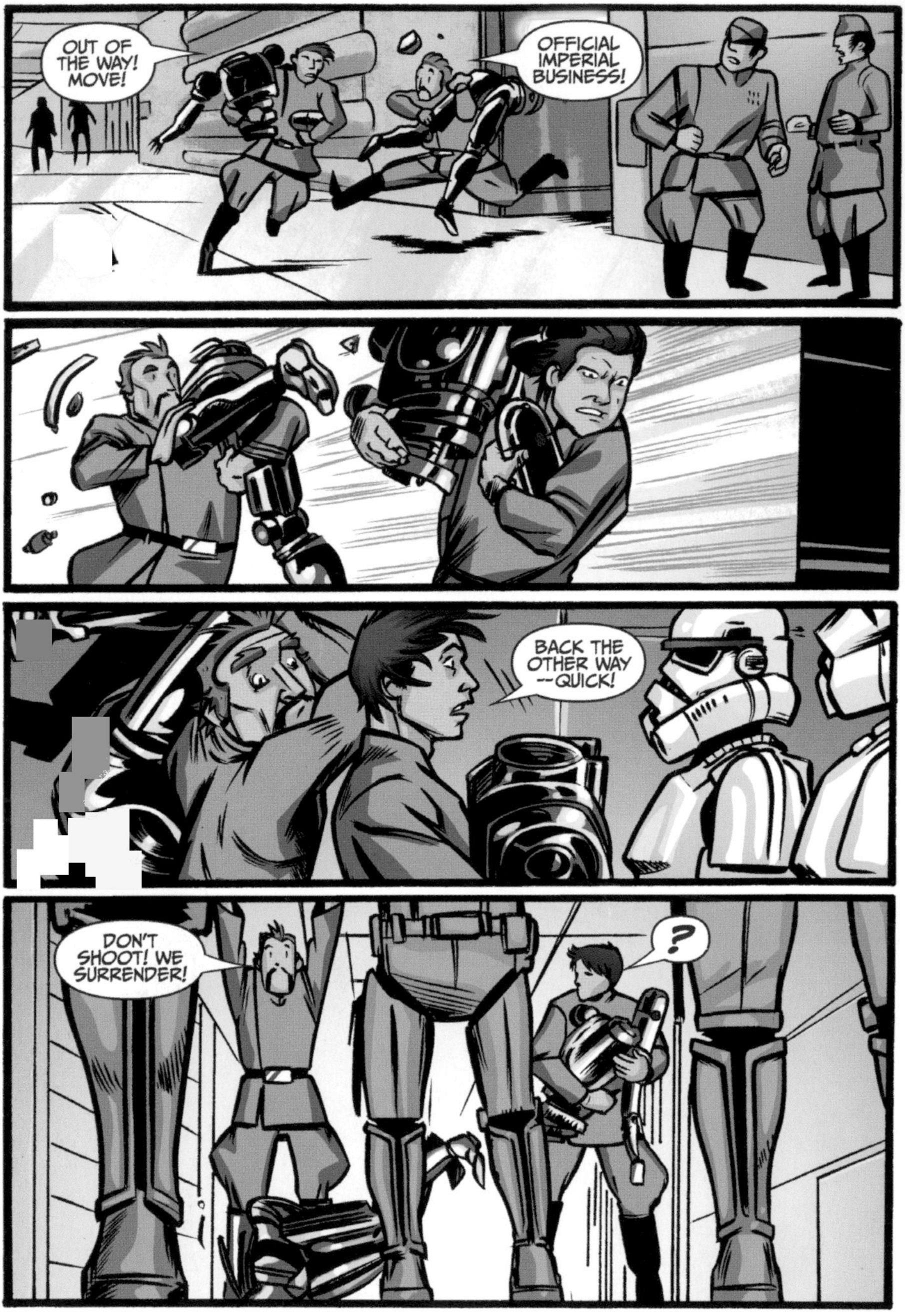
OUT OF THE WAY! MOVE!
OFFICIAL IMPERIAL BUSINESS!
BACK THE OTHER WAY --QUICK!
DON'T SHOOT! WE SURRENDER!
?

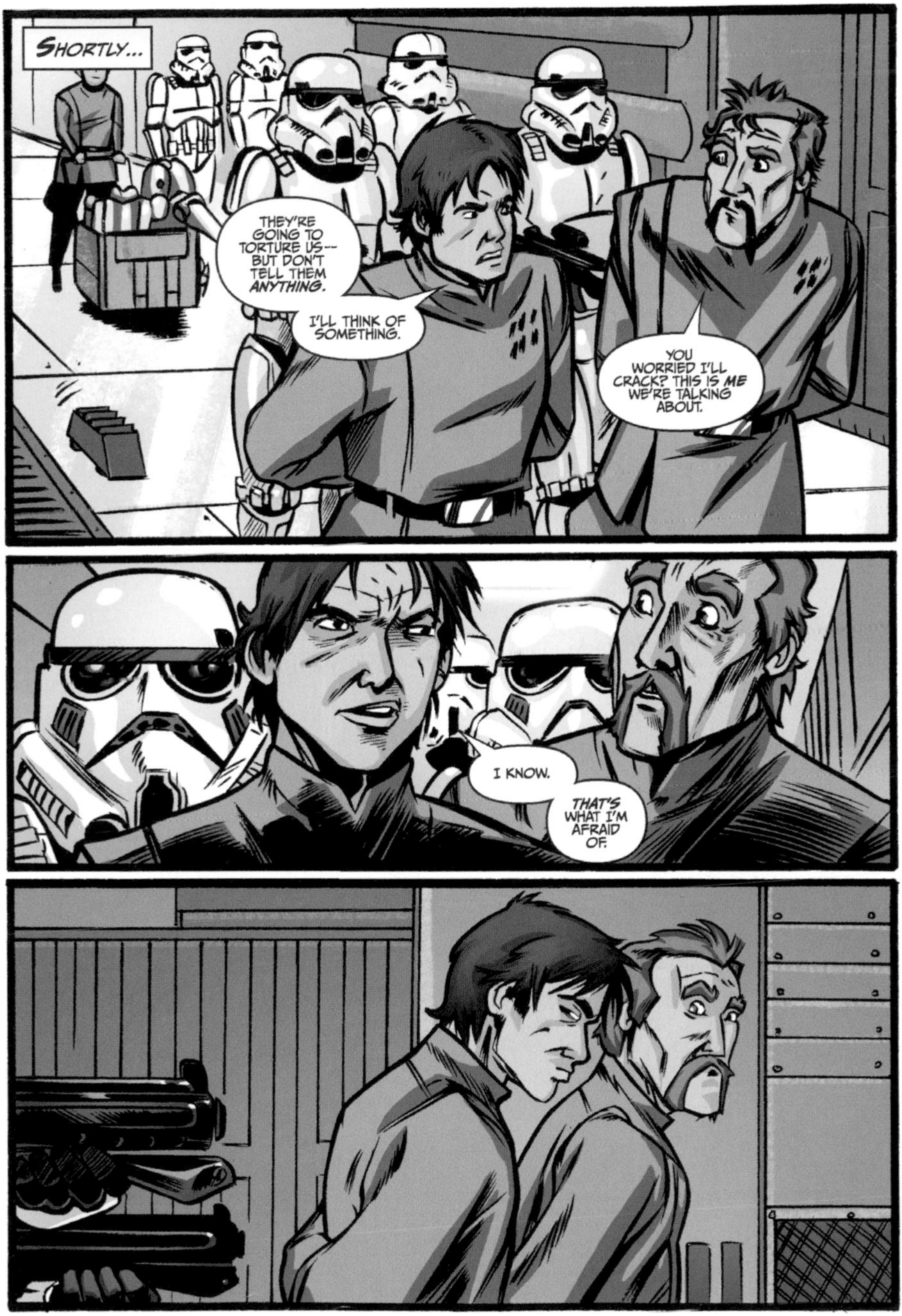
SHORTLY...
THEY'RE GOING TO TORTURE US-- BUT DON'T TELL THEM ANYTHING.
I'LL THINK OF SOMETHING.
YOU WORRIED I'LL CRACK? THIS IS ME WE'RE TALKING ABOUT.
I KNOW.
THAT'S WHAT I'M AFRAID OF.

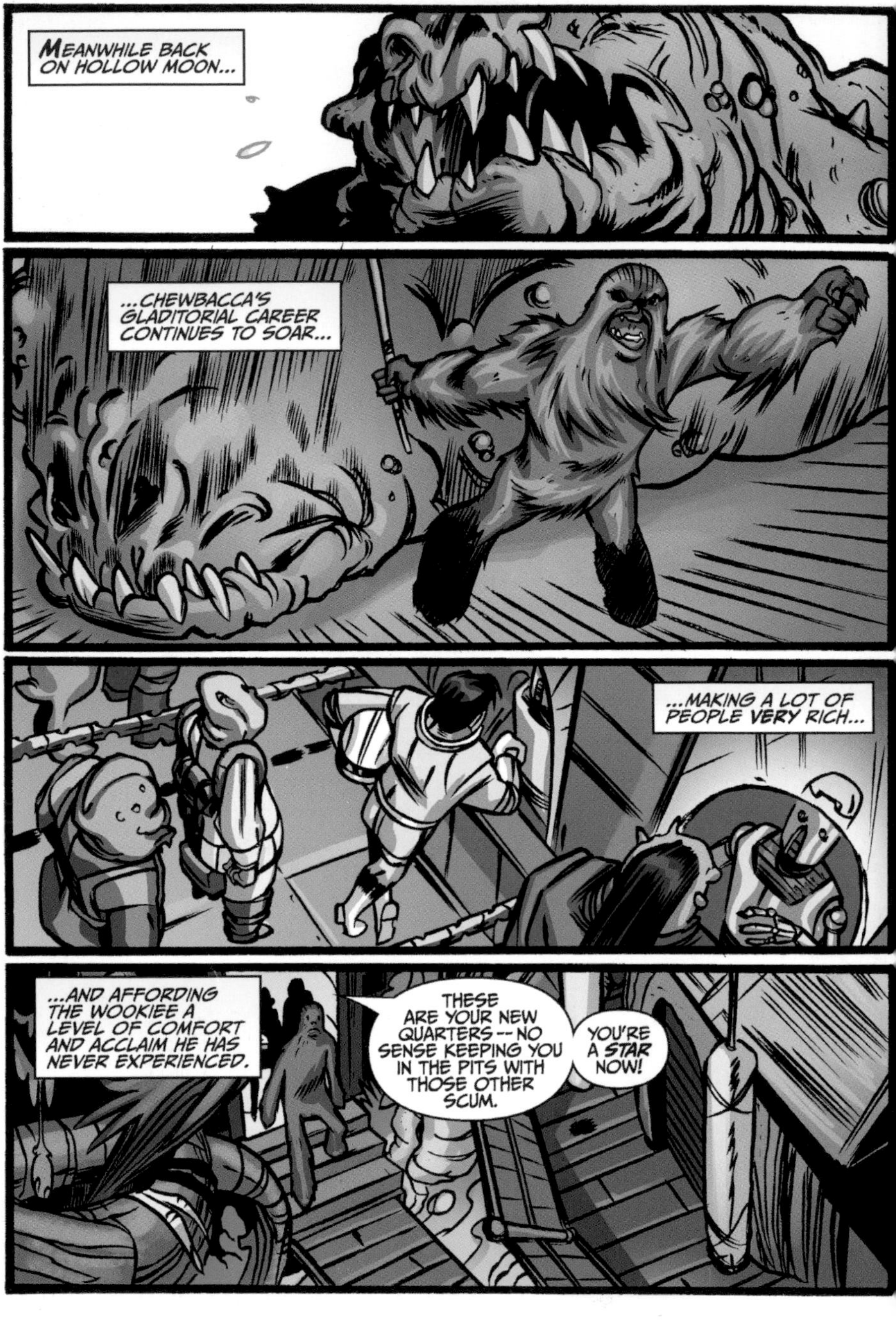
MEANWHILE BACK ON HOLLOW MOON...
...CHEWBACCA'S GLADITORIAL CAREER CONTINUES TO SOAR...
...MAKING A LOT OF PEOPLE VERY RICH...
...AND AFFORDING THE WOOKIEE A LEVEL OF COMFORT AND ACCLAIM HE HAS NEVER EXPERIENCED.
THESE ARE YOUR NEW QUARTERS--NO SENSE KEEPING YOU IN THE PITS WITH THOSE OTHER SCUM.
YOU'RE A STAR NOW!

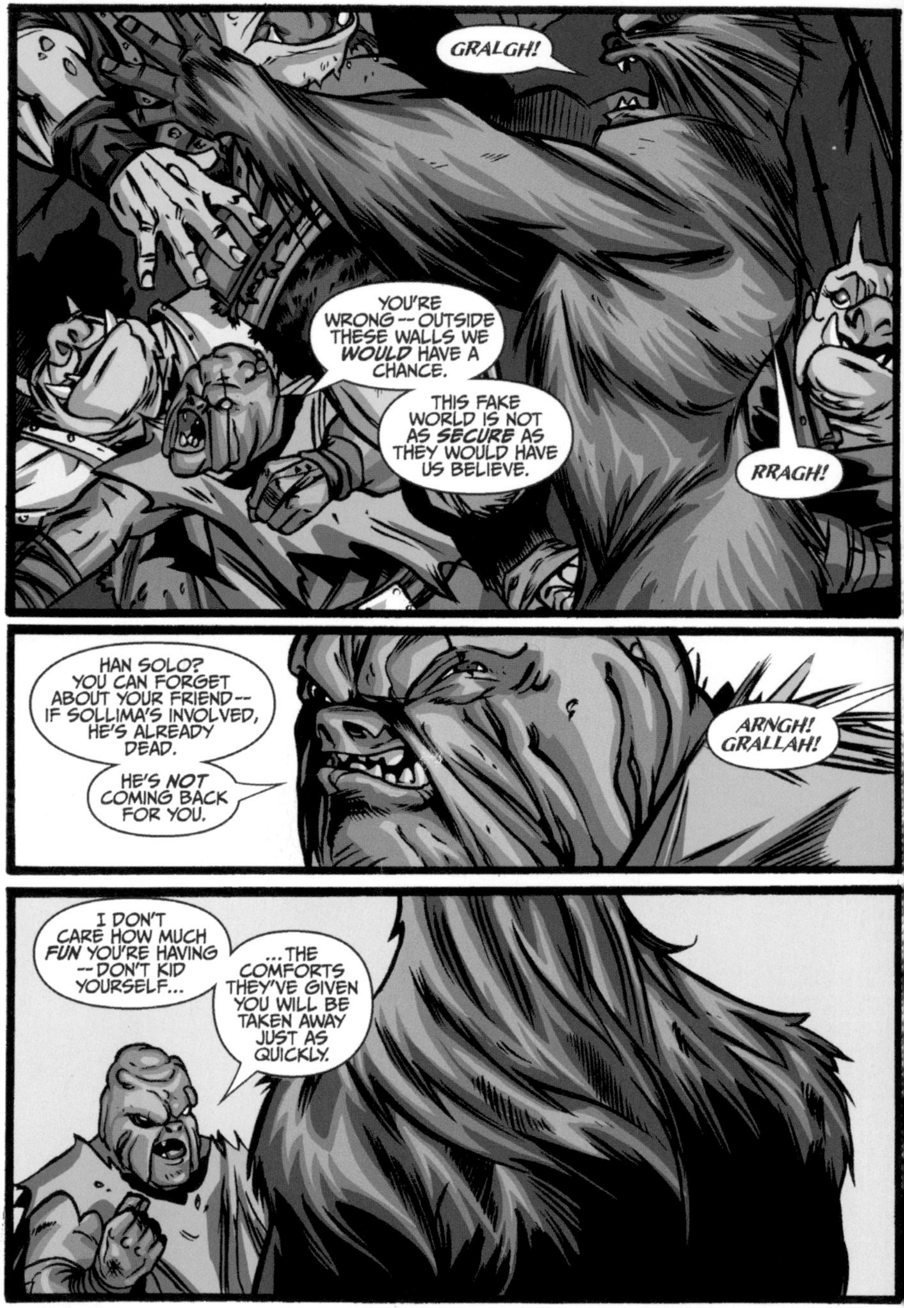
GRALGH!
YOU'RE WRONG--OUTSIDE THESE WALLS WE WOULD HAVE A CHANCE.
THIS FAKE WORLD IS NOT AS SECURE AS THEY WOULD HAVE US BELIEVE.
RRAGH!
HAN SOLO? YOU CAN FORGET ABOUT YOUR FRIEND--IF SOLLIMA'S INVOLVED, HE'S ALREADY DEAD.
HE'S NOT COMING BACK FOR YOU.
ARNGH! GRALLAH!
I DON'T CARE HOW MUCH FUN YOU'RE HAVING --DON'T KID YOURSELF...
...THE COMFORTS THEY'VE GIVEN YOU WILL BE TAKEN AWAY JUST AS QUICKLY.

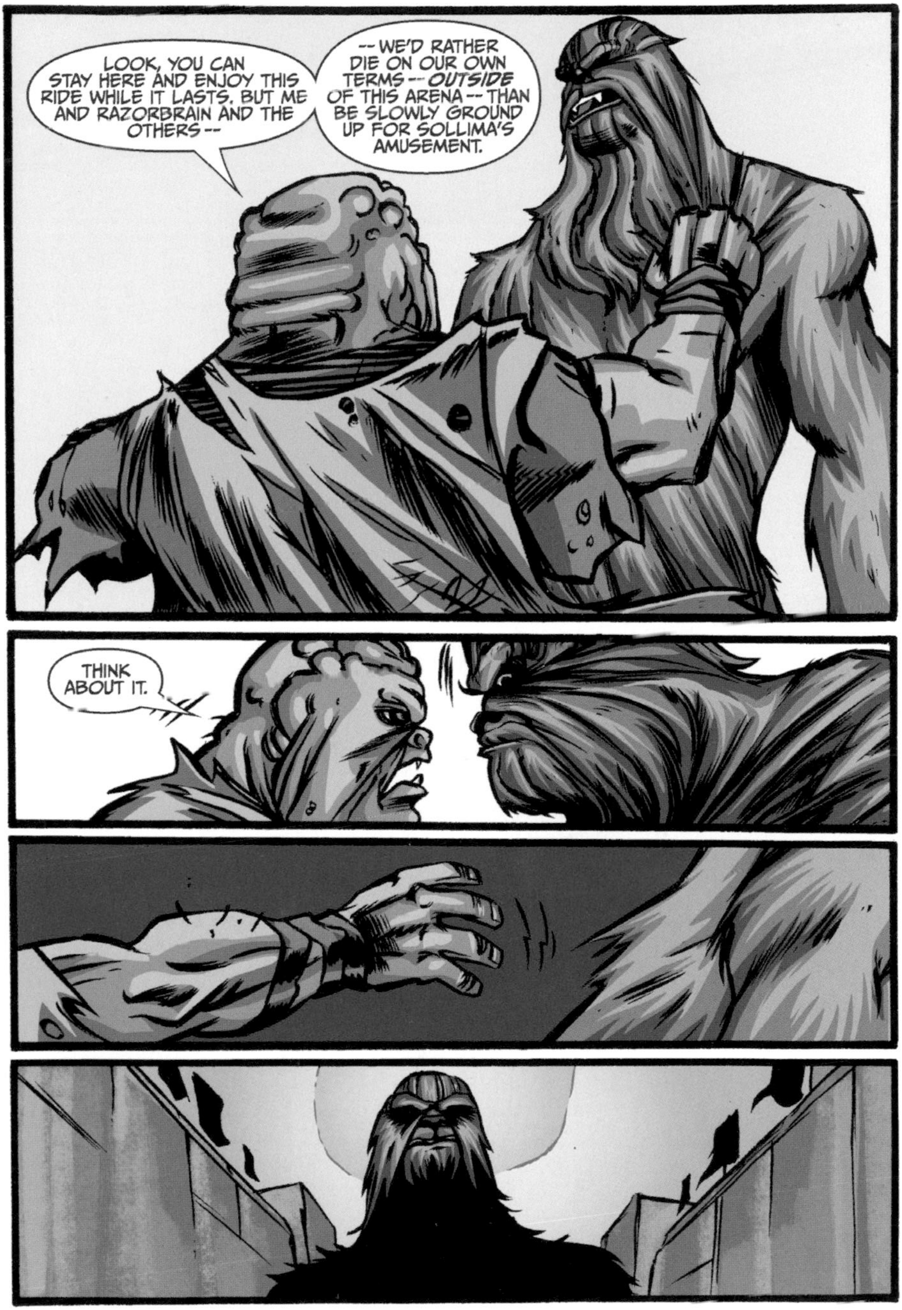
LOOK, YOU CAN STAY HERE AND ENJOY THIS RIDE WHILE IT LASTS. BUT ME AND RAZORBRAIN AND THE OTHERS--
--WE'D RATHER DIE ON OUR OWN TERMS--*OUTSIDE* OF THIS ARENA--THAN BE SLOWLY GROUND UP FOR SOLLIMA'S AMUSEMENT.
THINK ABOUT IT.

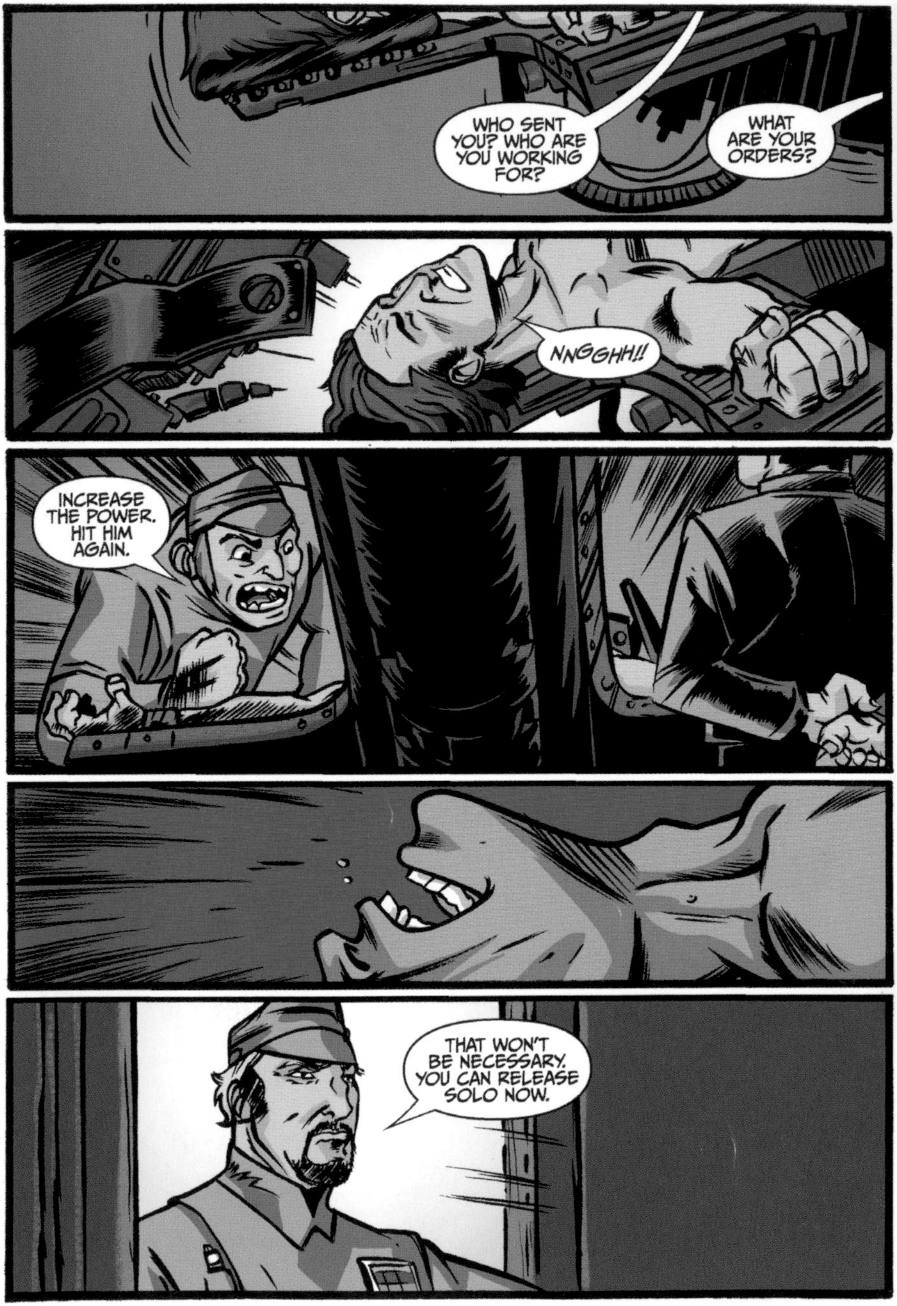

WHO SENT YOU? WHO ARE YOU WORKING FOR?
WHAT ARE YOUR ORDERS?
NNGGHH!!
INCREASE THE POWER. HIT HIM AGAIN.
THAT WON'T BE NECESSARY. YOU CAN RELEASE SOLO NOW.

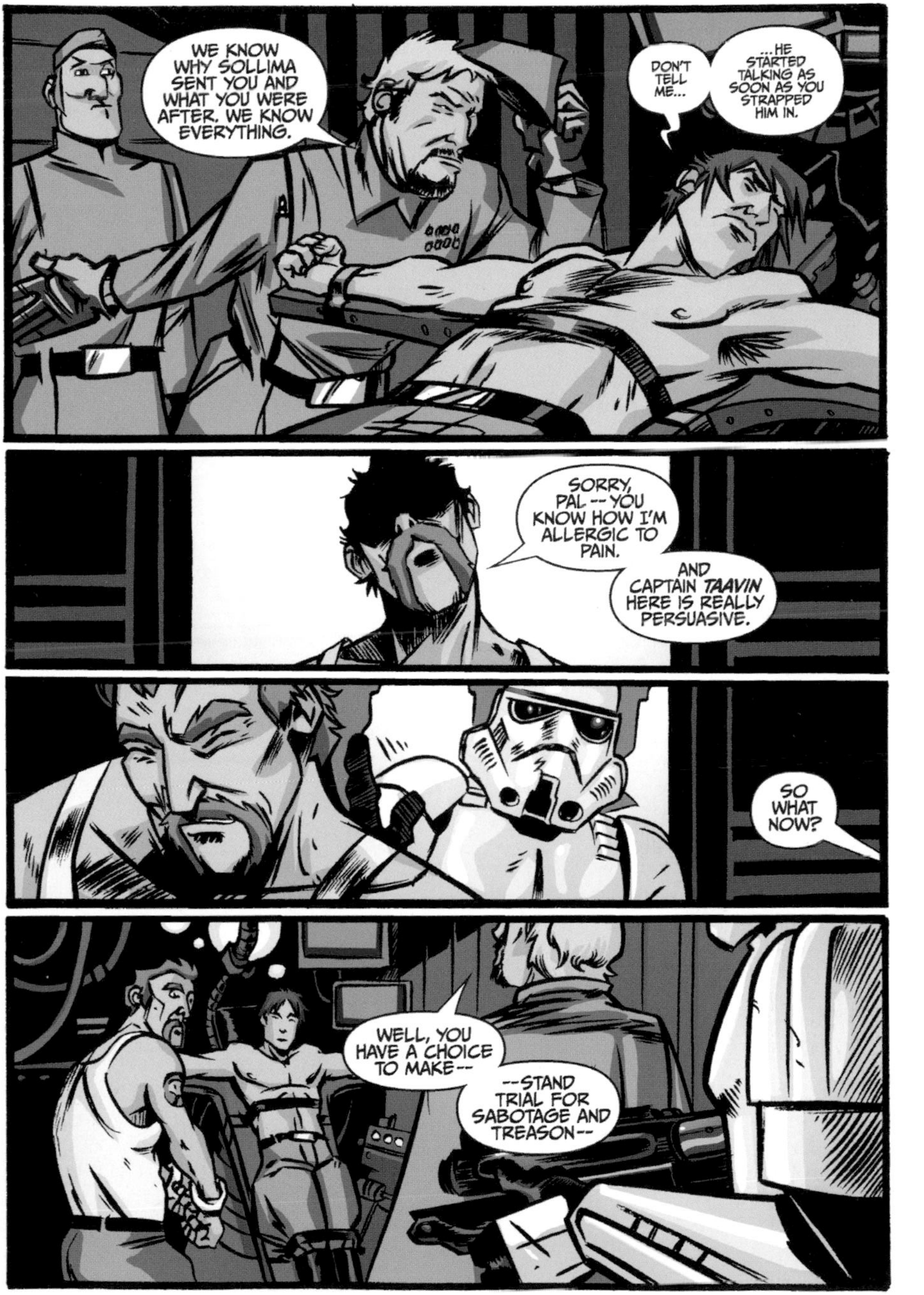
WE KNOW WHY SOLLIMA SENT YOU AND WHAT YOU WERE AFTER. WE KNOW EVERYTHING.
DON'T TELL ME...
...HE STARTED TALKING AS SOON AS YOU STRAPPED HIM IN.
SORRY, PAL -- YOU KNOW HOW I'M ALLERGIC TO PAIN.
AND CAPTAIN *TAAVIN* HERE IS REALLY PERSUASIVE.
SO WHAT NOW?
WELL, YOU HAVE A CHOICE TO MAKE--
--STAND TRIAL FOR SABOTAGE AND TREASON--

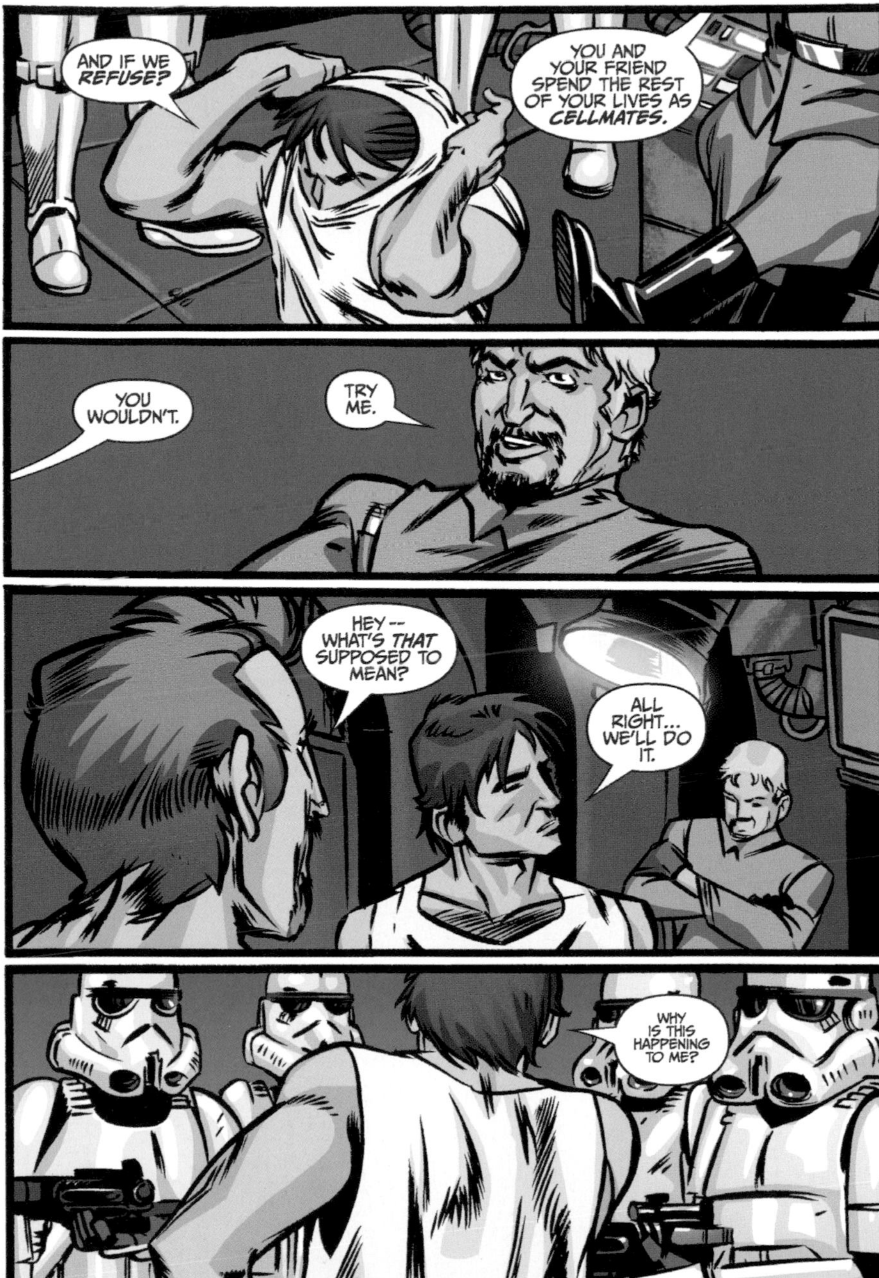
AND IF WE *REFUSE?*
YOU AND YOUR FRIEND SPEND THE REST OF YOUR LIVES AS *CELLMATES.*
YOU WOULDN'T.
TRY ME.
HEY -- WHAT'S *THAT* SUPPOSED TO MEAN?
ALL RIGHT... WE'LL DO IT.
WHY IS THIS HAPPENING TO ME?

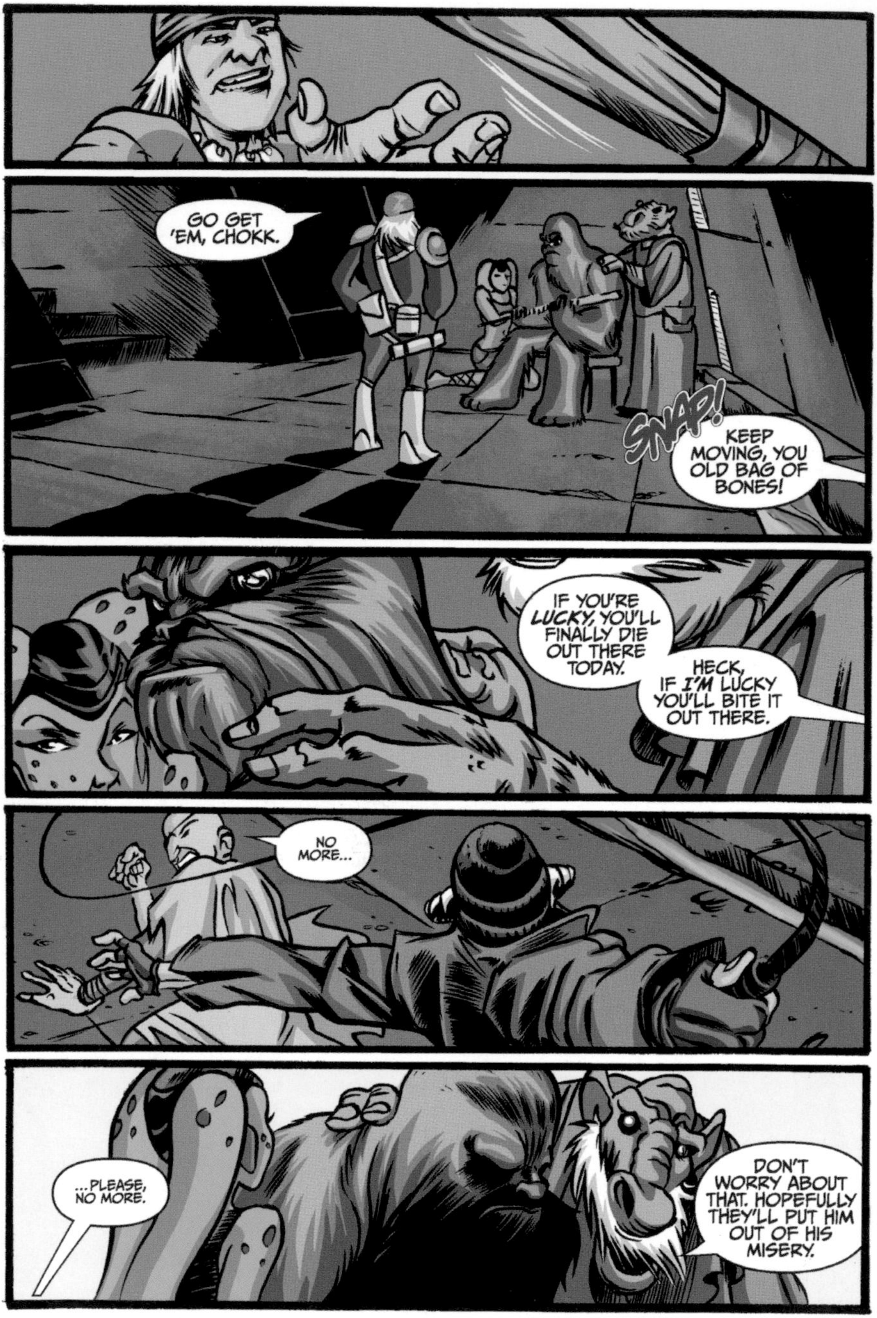
GO GET 'EM, CHOKK.
SNAP!
KEEP MOVING, YOU OLD BAG OF BONES!
IF YOU'RE *LUCKY,* YOU'LL FINALLY DIE OUT THERE TODAY.
HECK, IF *I'M* LUCKY YOU'LL BITE IT OUT THERE.
NO MORE...
...PLEASE, NO MORE.
DON'T WORRY ABOUT THAT. HOPEFULLY THEY'LL PUT HIM OUT OF HIS MISERY.

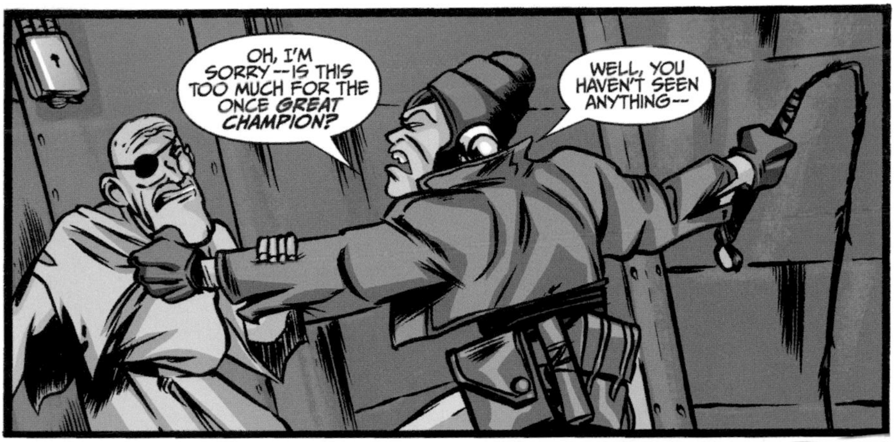
OH, I'M SORRY--IS THIS TOO MUCH FOR THE ONCE GREAT CHAMPION?
WELL, YOU HAVEN'T SEEN ANYTHING--
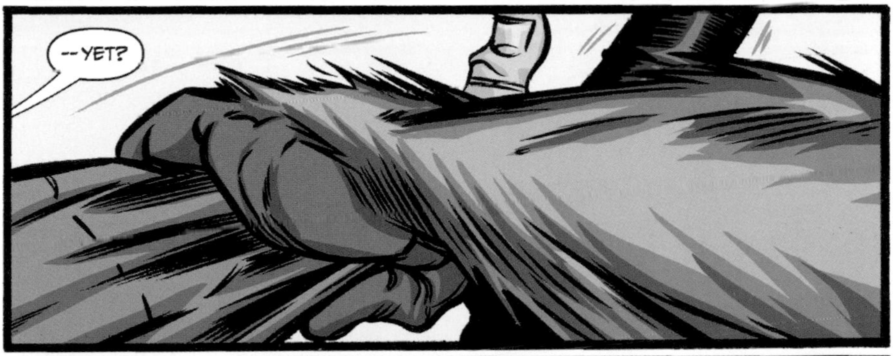
--YET?
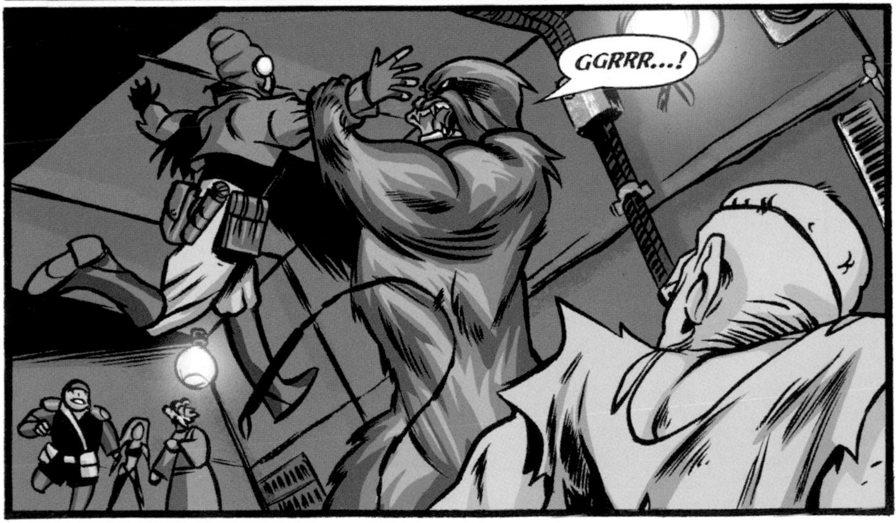
GGRRR...!

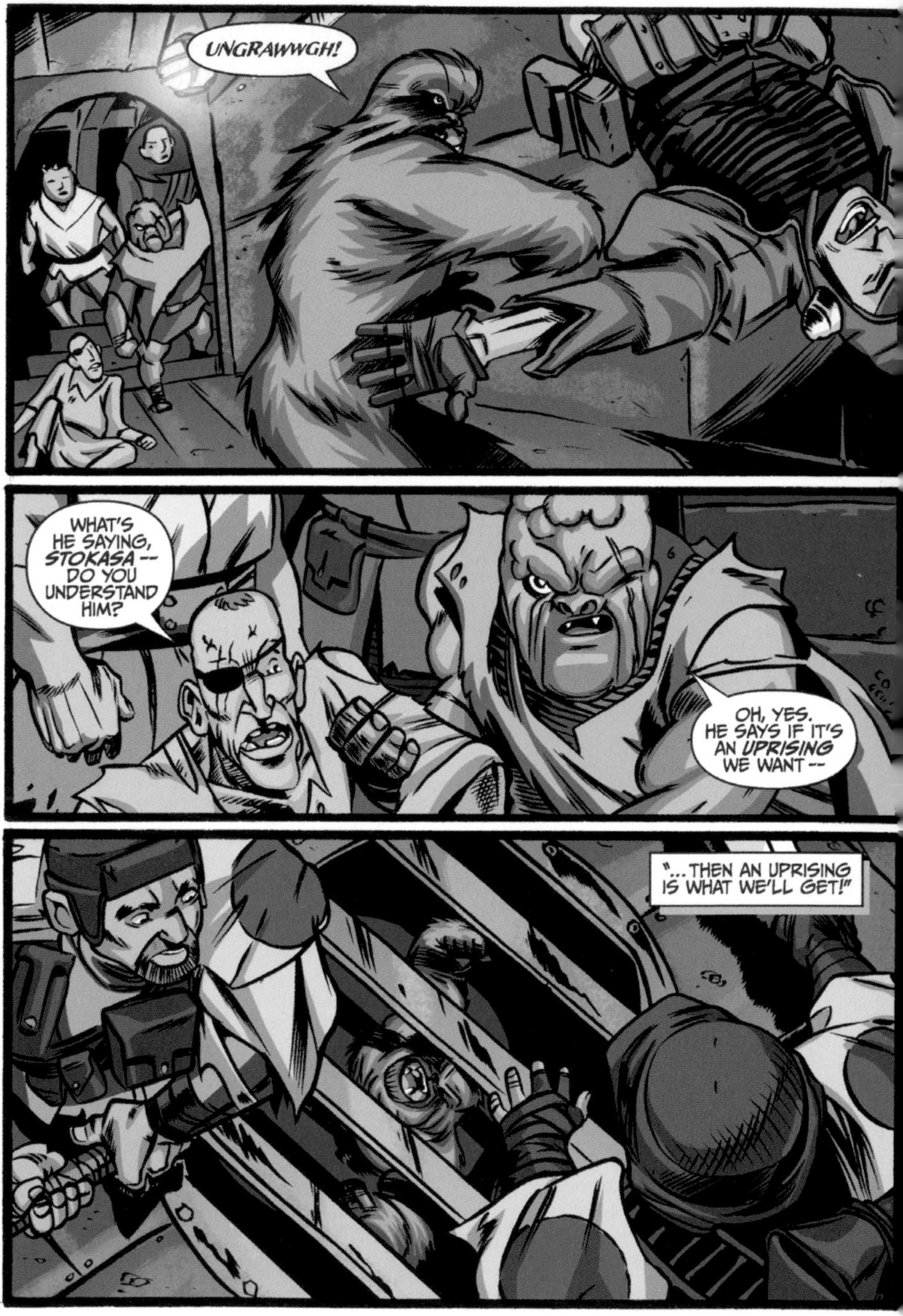
UNGRAWWGH!
WHAT'S HE SAYING, STOKASA -- DO YOU UNDERSTAND HIM?
OH, YES. HE SAYS IF IT'S AN UPRISING WE WANT --
"...THEN AN UPRISING IS WHAT WE'LL GET!"

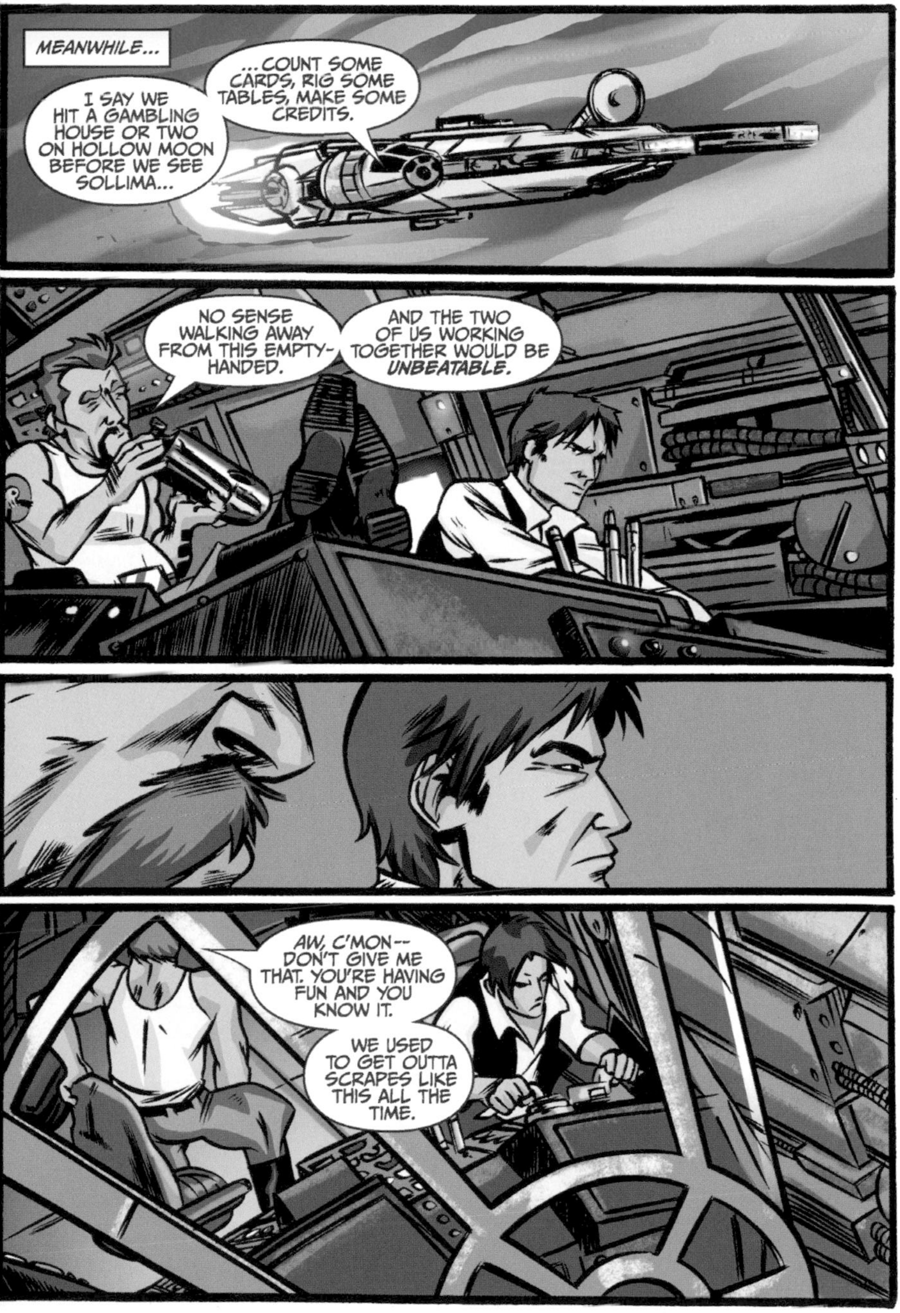
MEANWHILE...
I SAY WE HIT A GAMBLING HOUSE OR TWO ON HOLLOW MOON BEFORE WE SEE SOLLIMA...
...COUNT SOME CARDS, RIG SOME TABLES, MAKE SOME CREDITS.
NO SENSE WALKING AWAY FROM THIS EMPTY-HANDED.
AND THE TWO OF US WORKING TOGETHER WOULD BE *UNBEATABLE.*
AW, C'MON-- DON'T GIVE ME THAT. YOU'RE HAVING FUN AND YOU KNOW IT.
WE USED TO GET OUTTA SCRAPES LIKE THIS ALL THE TIME.

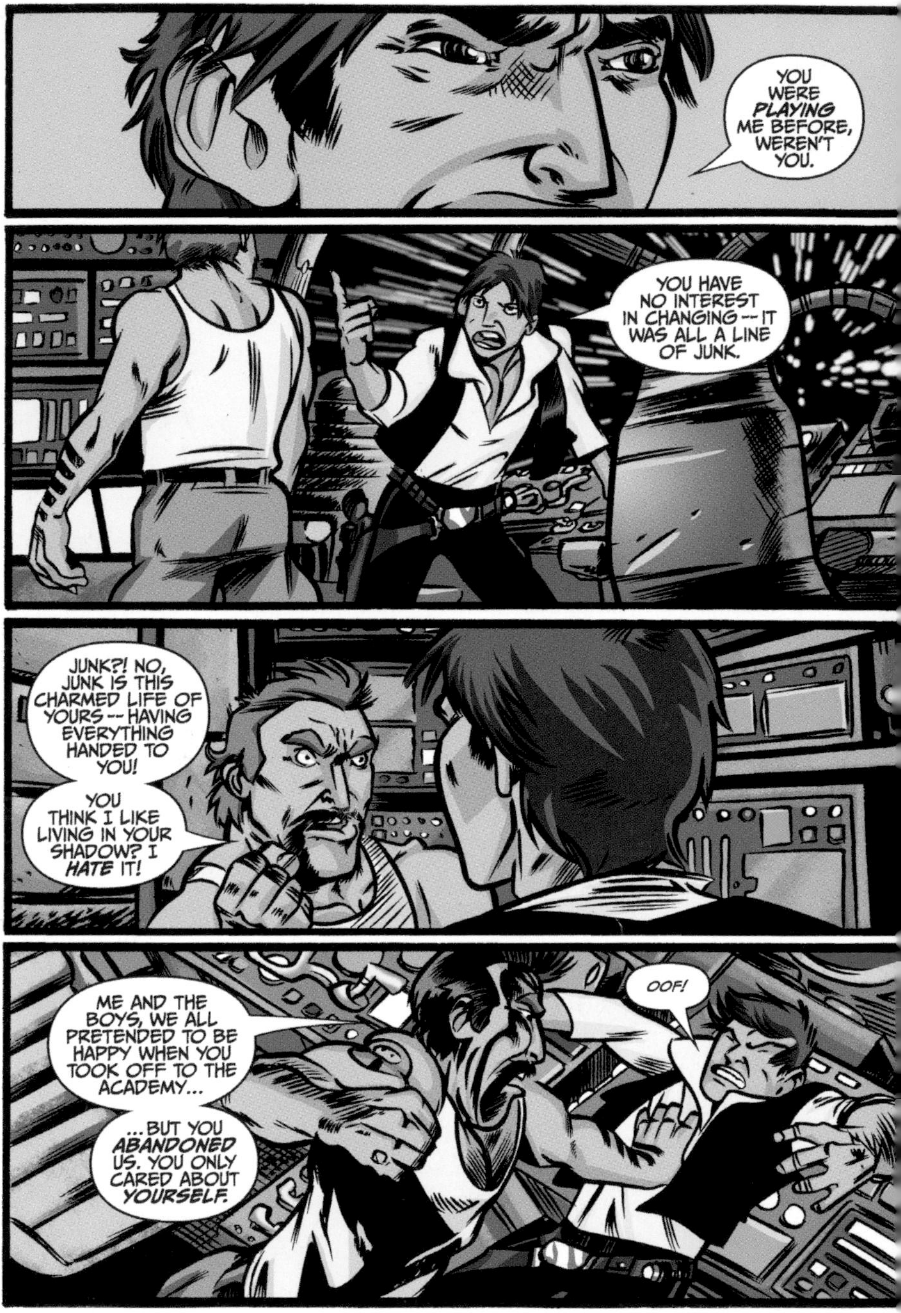
YOU WERE PLAYING ME BEFORE, WEREN'T YOU.
YOU HAVE NO INTEREST IN CHANGING -- IT WAS ALL A LINE OF JUNK.
JUNK?! NO, JUNK IS THIS CHARMED LIFE OF YOURS -- HAVING EVERYTHING HANDED TO YOU!
YOU THINK I LIKE LIVING IN YOUR SHADOW? I HATE IT!
ME AND THE BOYS, WE ALL PRETENDED TO BE HAPPY WHEN YOU TOOK OFF TO THE ACADEMY...
...BUT YOU ABANDONED US. YOU ONLY CARED ABOUT YOURSELF.
OOF!

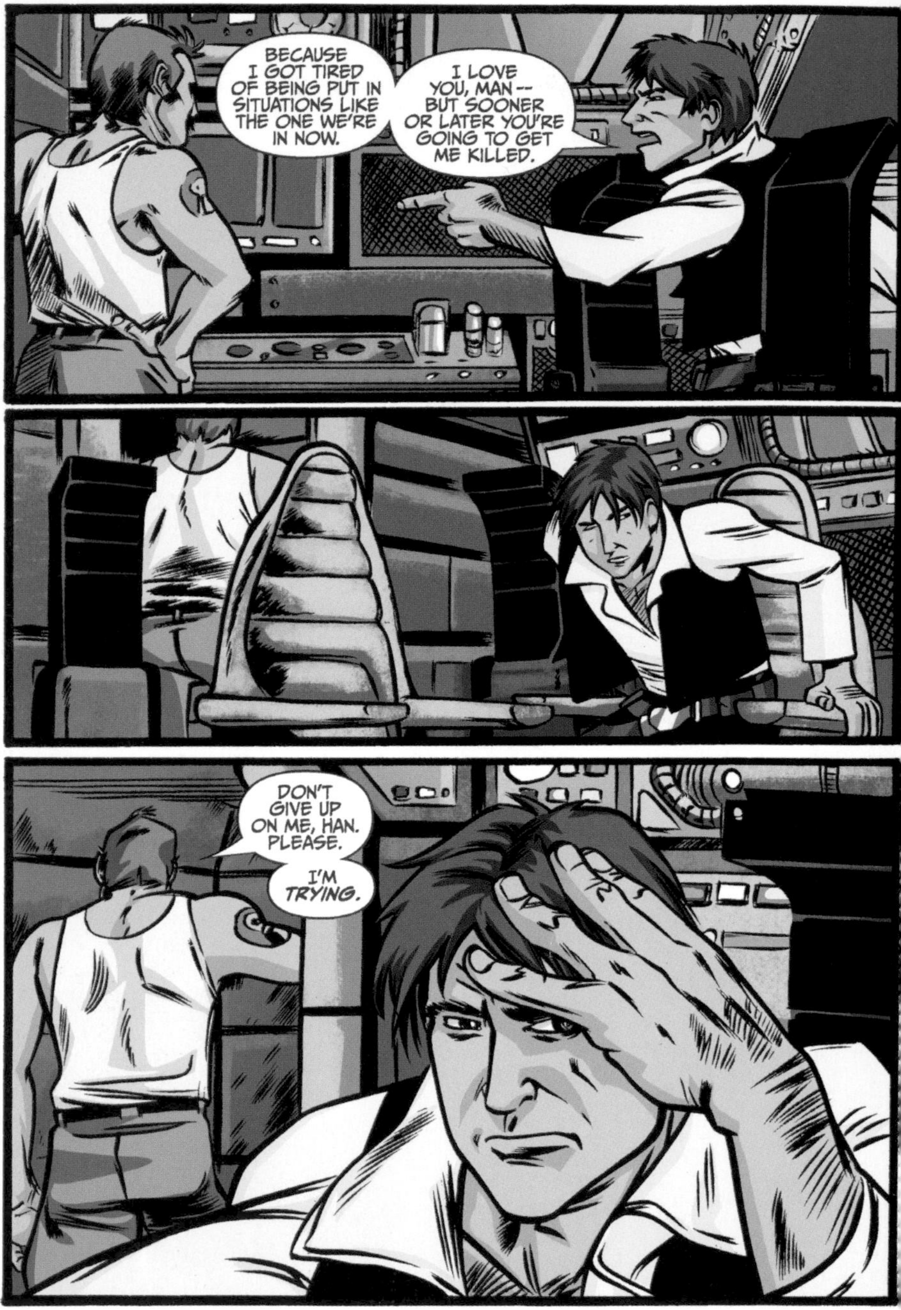
BECAUSE I GOT TIRED OF BEING PUT IN SITUATIONS LIKE THE ONE WE'RE IN NOW.
I LOVE YOU, MAN-- BUT SOONER OR LATER YOU'RE GOING TO GET ME KILLED.
DON'T GIVE UP ON ME, HAN. PLEASE.
I'M *TRYING.*

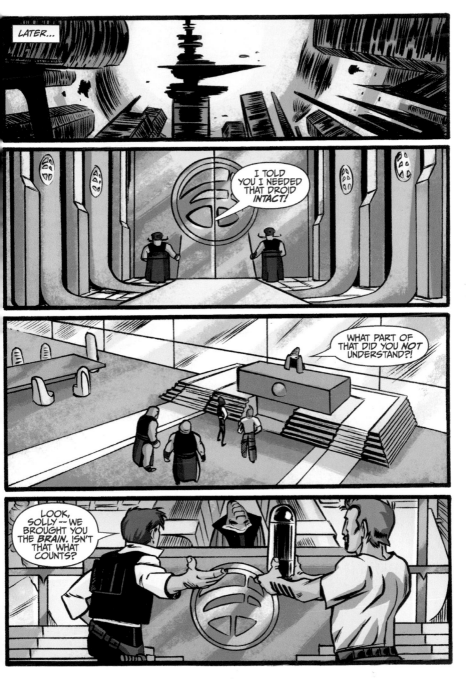

LATER...

I TOLD YOU I NEEDED THAT DROID INTACT!

WHAT PART OF THAT DID YOU *NOT* UNDERSTAND?!

LOOK, SOLLY -- WE BROUGHT YOU THE *BRAIN*. ISN'T THAT WHAT COUNTS?

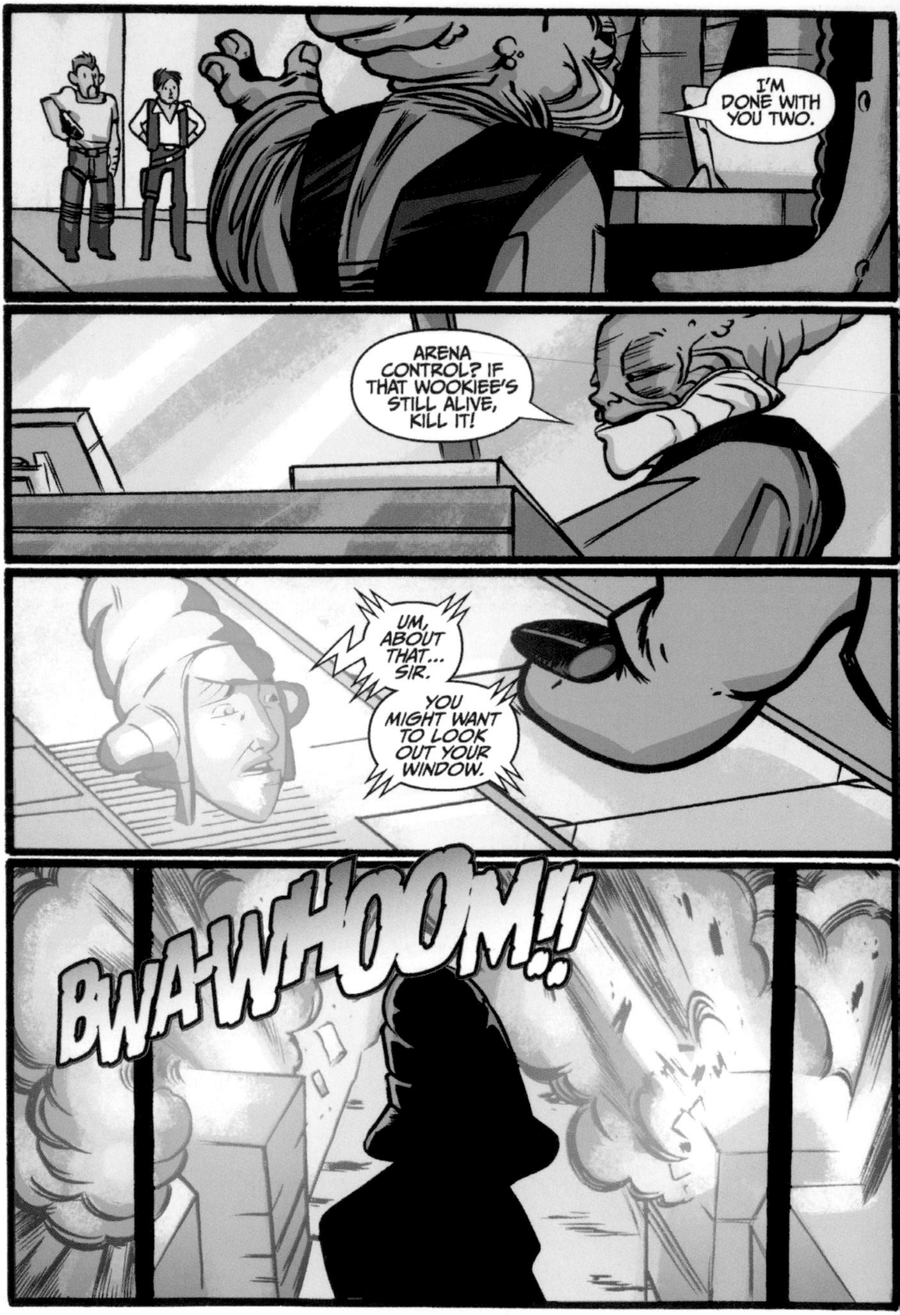
I'M DONE WITH YOU TWO.
ARENA CONTROL? IF THAT WOOKIEE'S STILL ALIVE, KILL IT!
UM, ABOUT THAT... SIR.
YOU MIGHT WANT TO LOOK OUT YOUR WINDOW.
BWAWHOOM!!

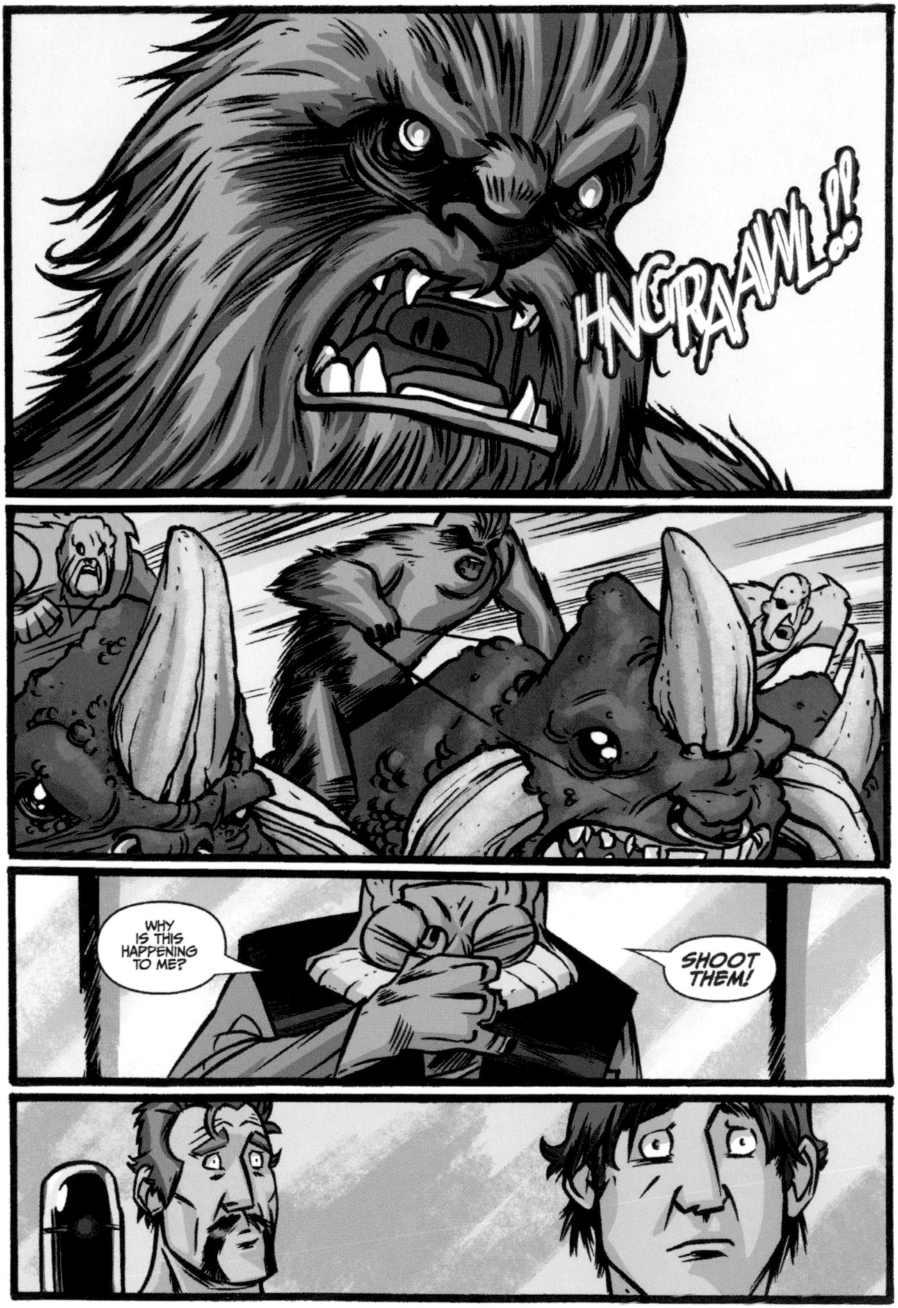
HNGRAAWL!!
WHY IS THIS HAPPENING TO ME?
SHOOT THEM!

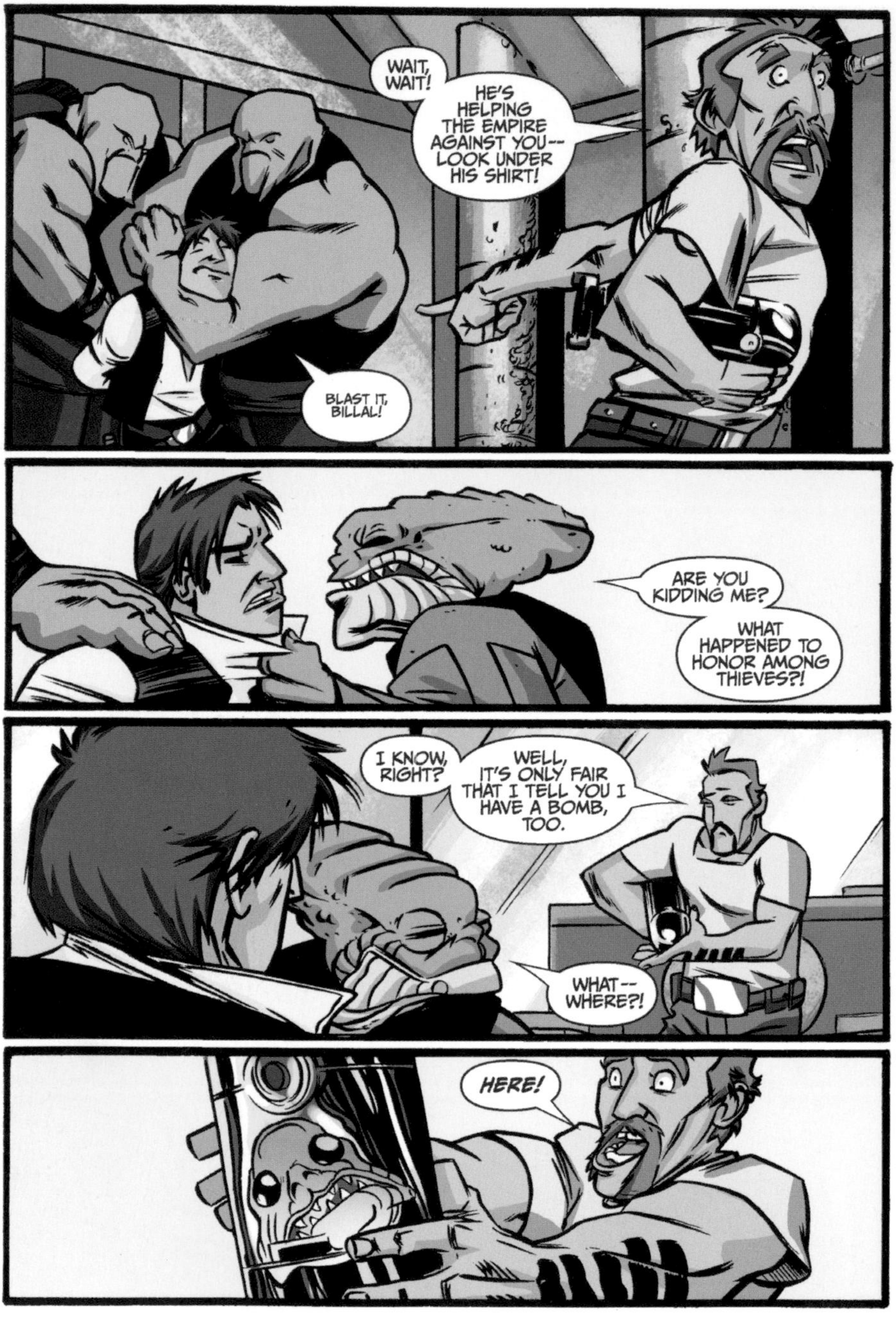
WAIT, WAIT!
HE'S HELPING THE EMPIRE AGAINST YOU-- LOOK UNDER HIS SHIRT!
BLAST IT, BILLAL!
ARE YOU KIDDING ME?
WHAT HAPPENED TO HONOR AMONG THIEVES?!
I KNOW, RIGHT?
WELL, IT'S ONLY FAIR THAT I TELL YOU I HAVE A BOMB, TOO.
WHAT-- WHERE?!
HERE!

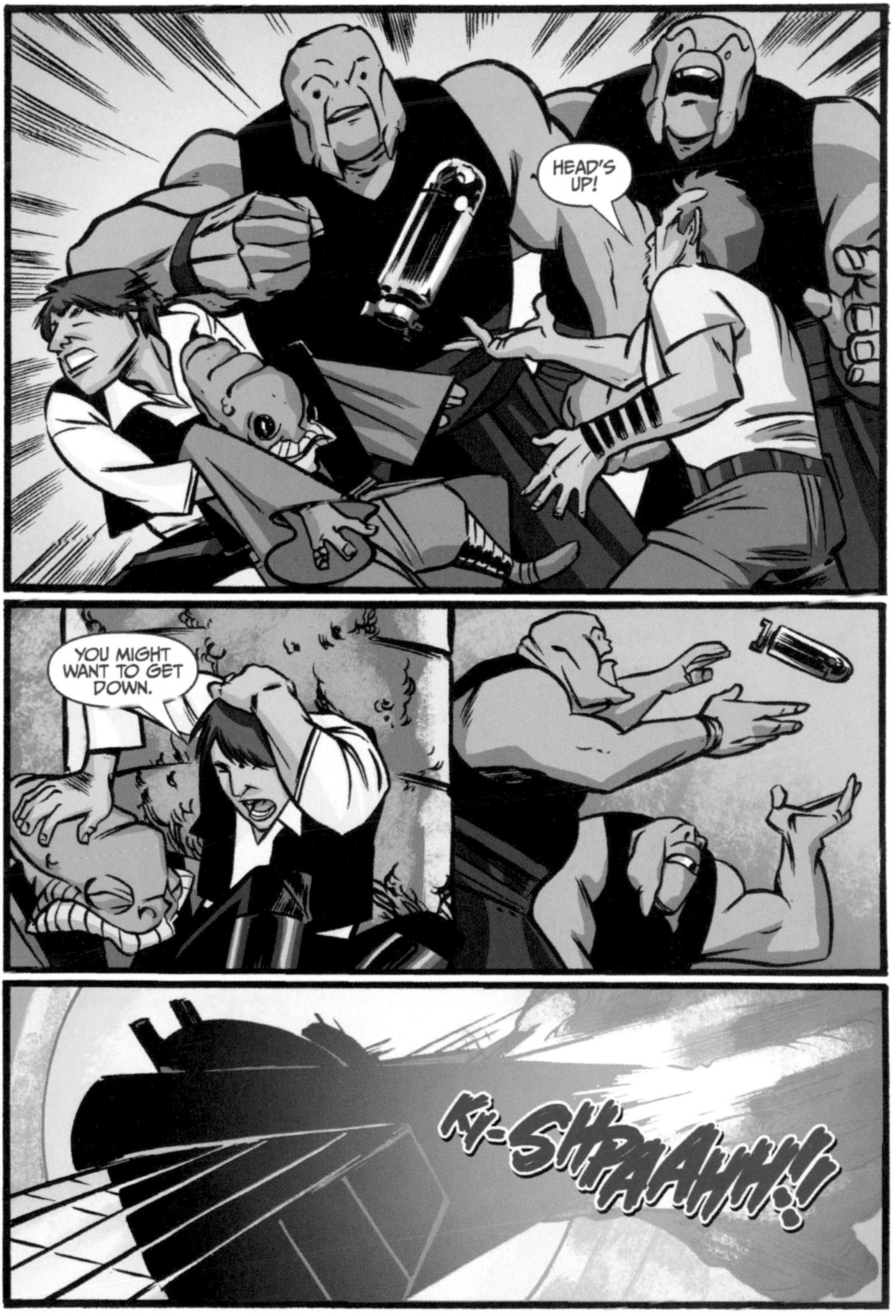
HEAD'S UP!
YOU MIGHT WANT TO GET DOWN.
KI-SHPAAHH!

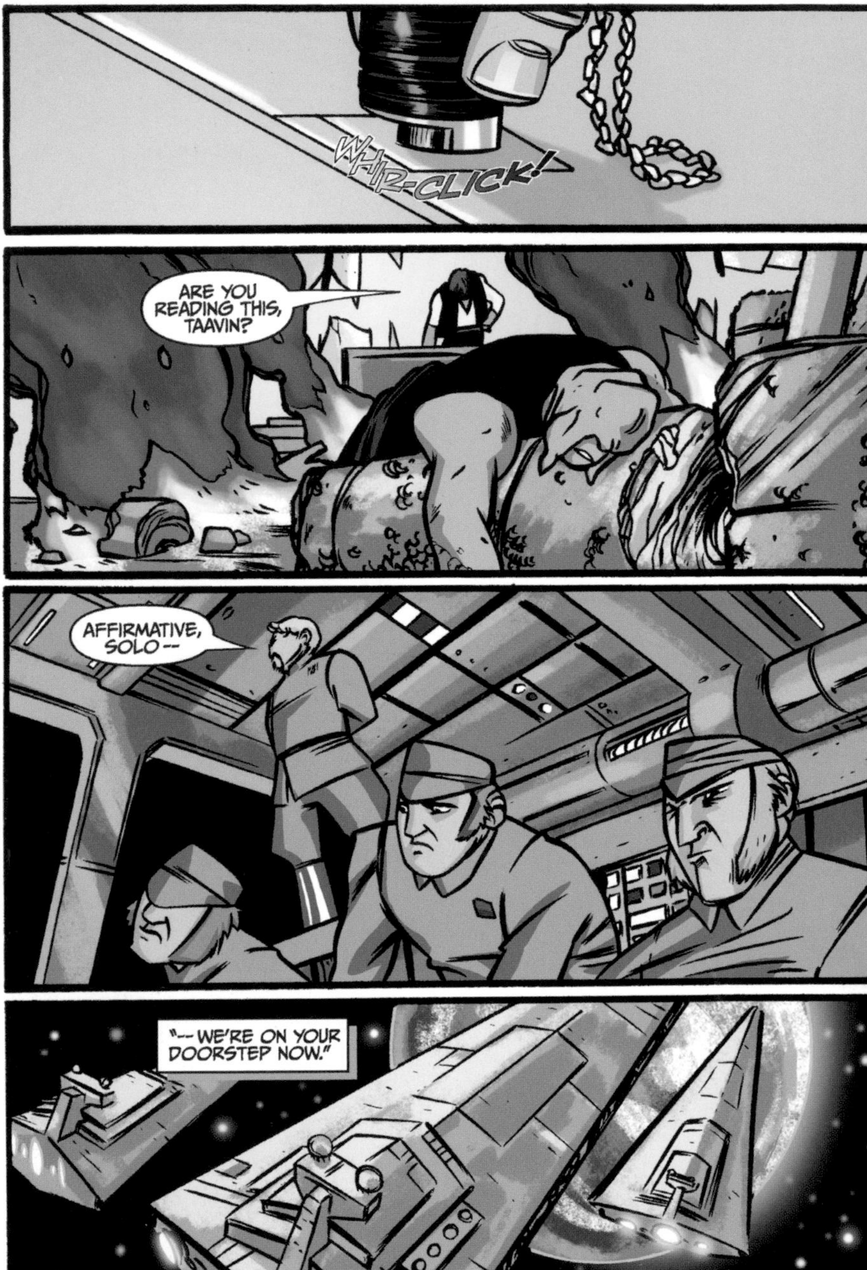
WHIR-CLICK!
ARE YOU READING THIS, TAAVIN?
AFFIRMATIVE, SOLO --
"-- WE'RE ON YOUR DOORSTEP NOW."

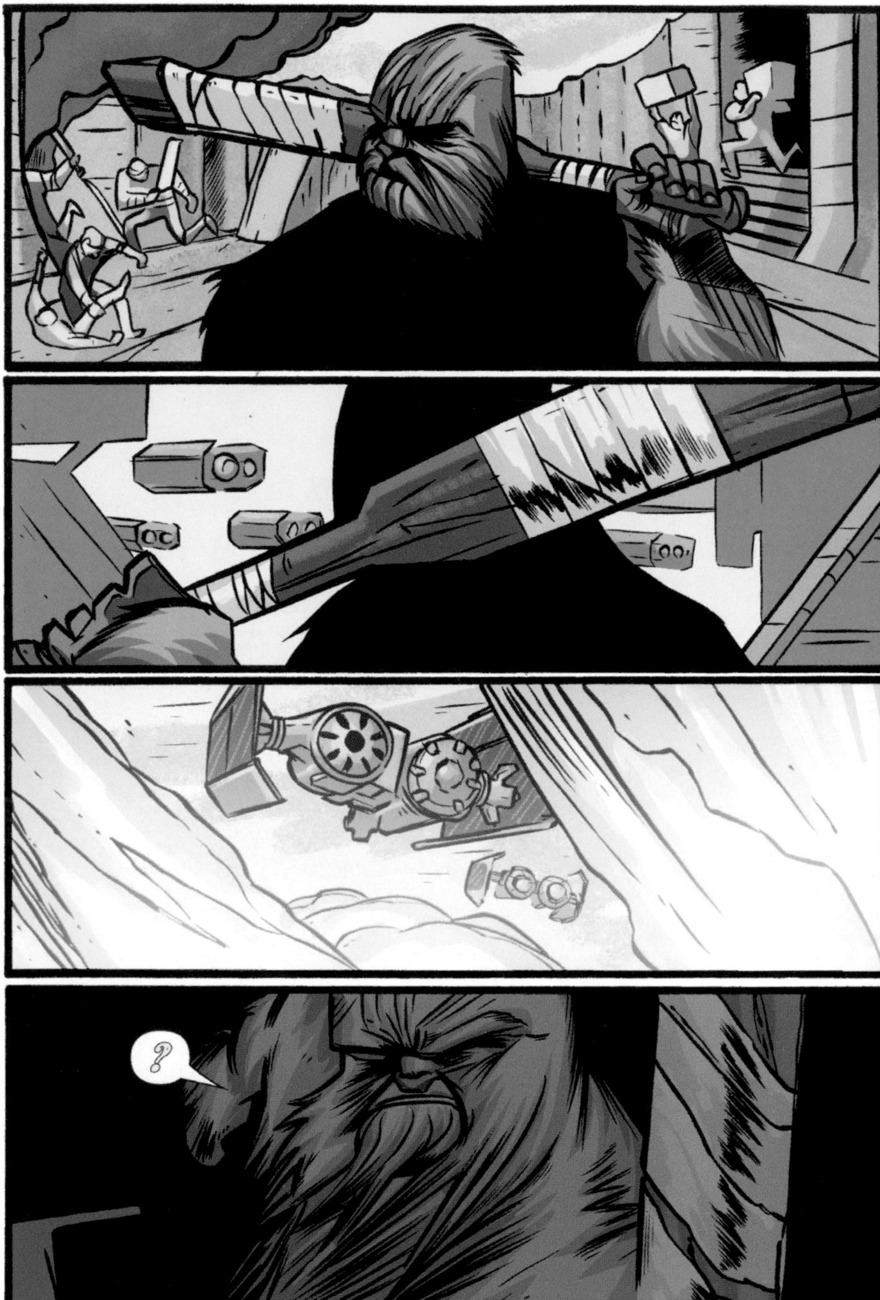
?

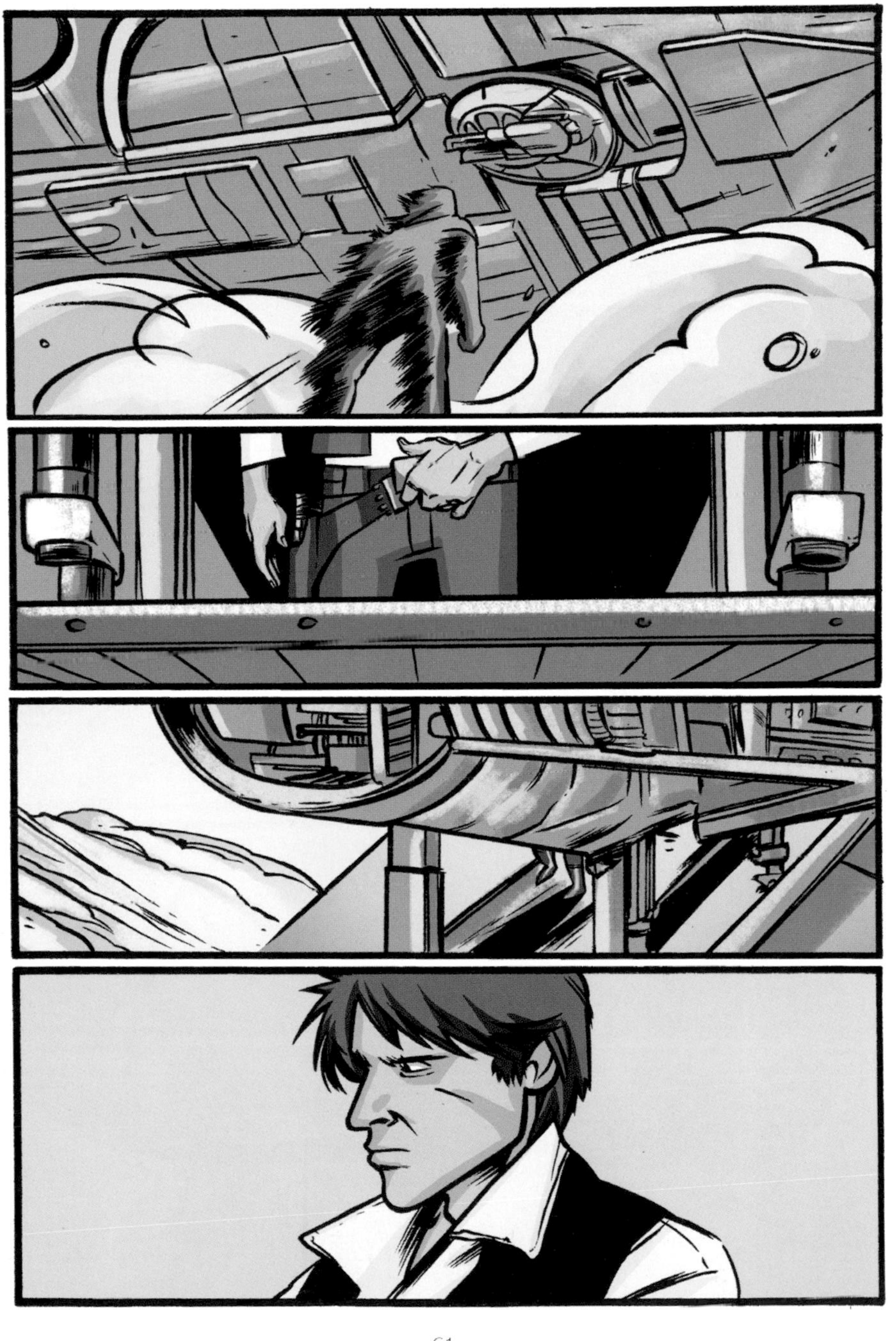

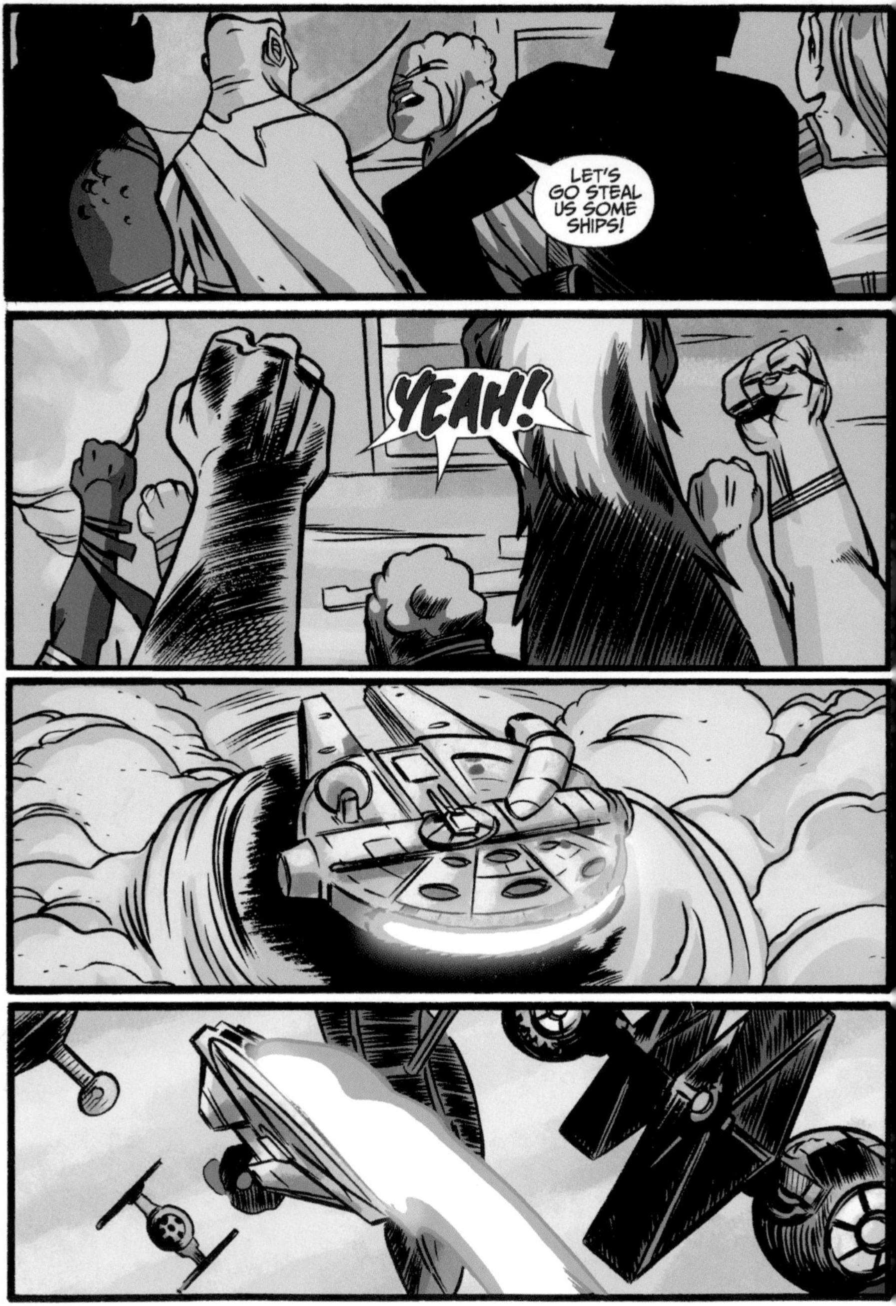
LET'S GO STEAL US SOME SHIPS!
YEAH!

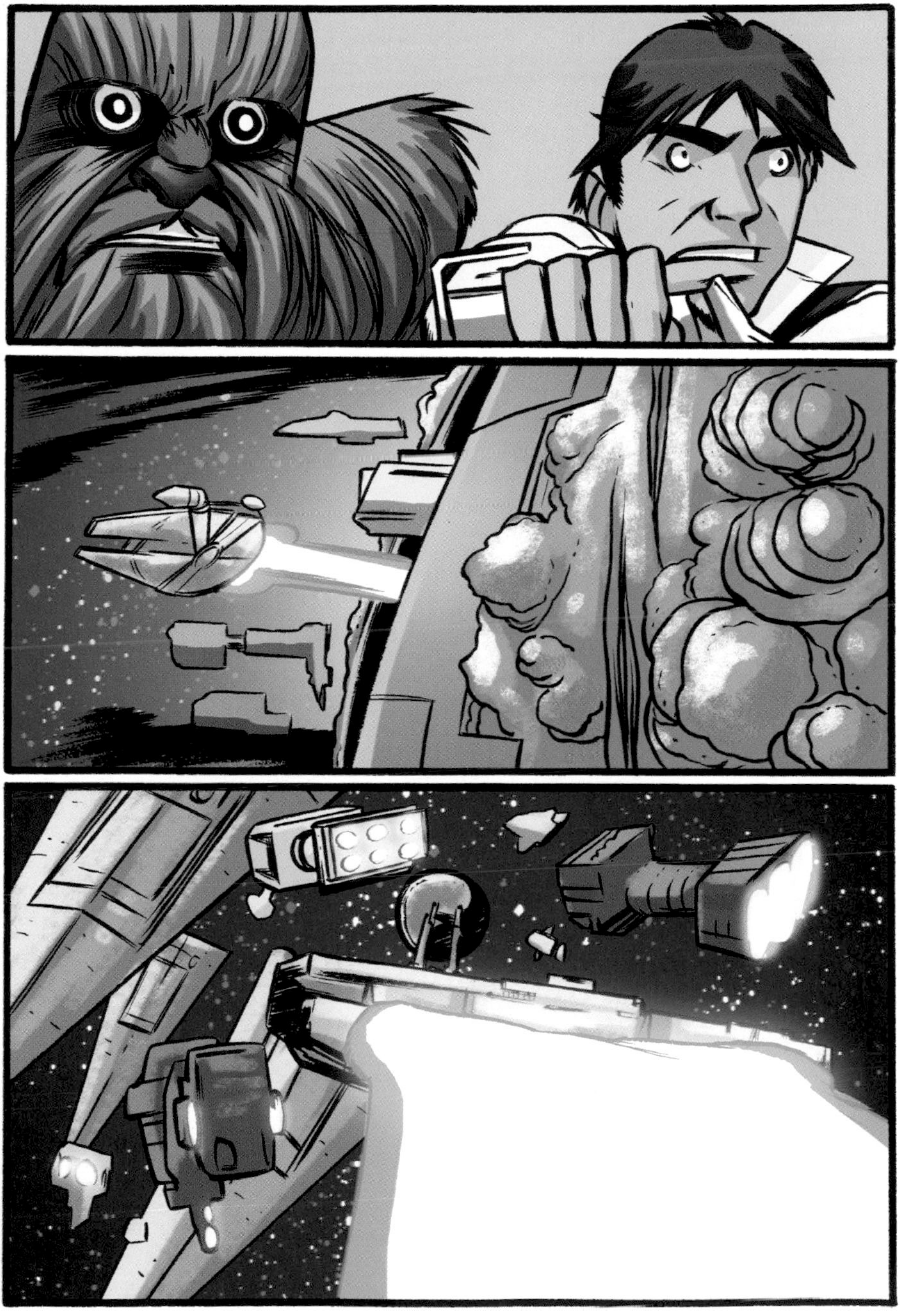

68

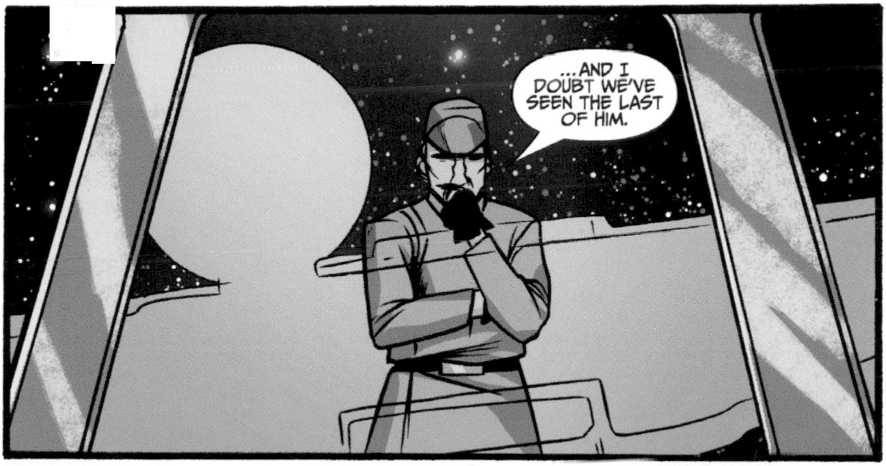
...AND I DOUBT WE'VE SEEN THE LAST OF HIM.

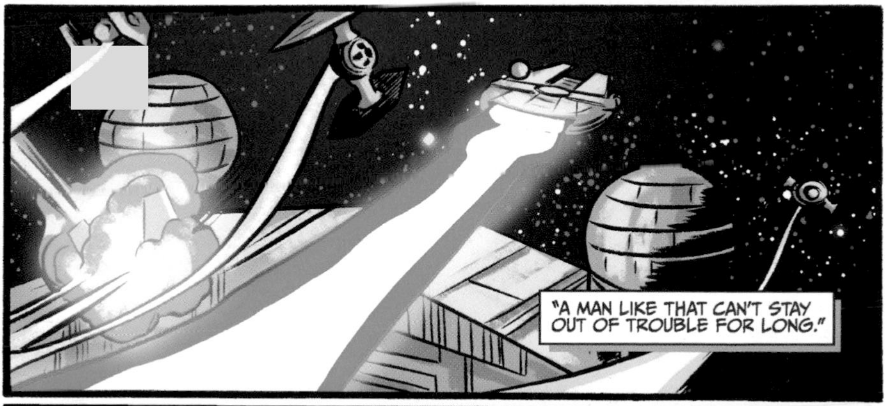
"A MAN LIKE THAT CAN'T STAY OUT OF TROUBLE FOR LONG."

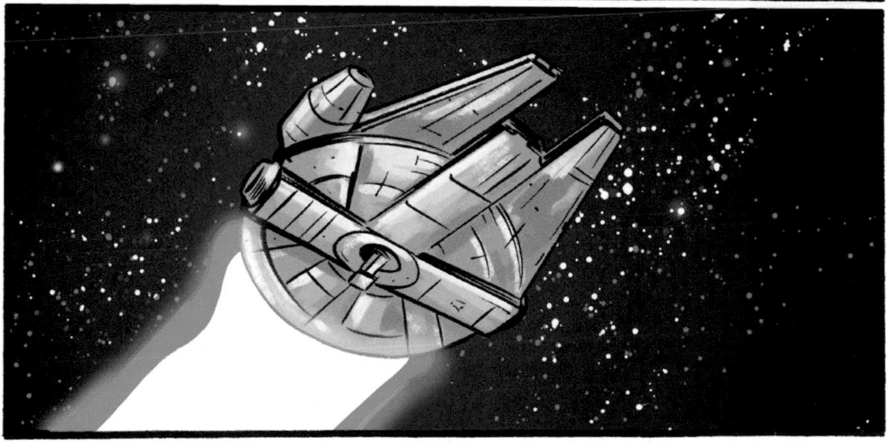